CADENCE REFLECTION

WHEELS & HOGS GARAGE
BOOK 2

D.M. EARL

Copyright
Copyright @ 2014 D. M. Earl

All rights reserved. Except for use in any review, the reproduction or utilization of this work in whole or in any part in any form by any electronic, mechanical or any other means, now or hereafter invented including photocopying, recording, information storage and retrieval systems-except in the case of brief quotations embodied in the critical article or reviews-without permission in writing from the author. This book may not be resold or redistributed without the express consent of the author.

For any questions or comments please email the author directly at DM@DMEARL.COM

This book is a work of fiction. All characters, events and places portrayed in this book are products of the author's imagination and are either fictitious or are used fictitiously. Any similarity to real persons, living or deceased is purely coincidental and not intentional.

This book contains sexual encounters, consensual and graphic language that some readers may find objectionable. It contains graphic material that is not suitable for anyone under the age of 18.

Romantic Erotic Mature Audience.

This book is dedicated to two very special men in my life, my husband and my lil brother.

To the man who has helped me find myself then proven time and time again that he believes in me, my husband and Best Friend, Chuck. Baby, you are the light that brings me from my own darkness. You allow me to run but you pull me back when I need it. You're always there to pick up the pieces no matter what, no questions asked. You are the reason my life is now complete as you are my other half. You are the only man I trust 100%. I love you, trust you, and need you more every day of my life.

To my little brother and closest friend whom I love unconditionally, I dedicate this book to you. We have been through hell and back and survived. Knowing you were there made it easier to get through. Your strength, tender heart, and humor over the years are what I love the most about you. Know how proud I am of you always. You were there when no one else was and supported me when I couldn't do it for myself. I am always here for you and will always have your back. I love you, Chet.

Finally, to our two "four-legged kids" Buddy & Chloe who we lost recently. We hope you are rolling in the grass, enjoying the sun shining on you, and enjoying each day after your final journey over the Rainbow Bridge. Mommy & Daddy love you and miss with all of our hearts.

CHAPTER ONE

CADENCE

As the nightmare begins, my body reacts. I start to tremble while grinding my teeth, moaning, and whimpering as if I'm in pain because in my nightmare I am in pain—so much pain. I reach up to cover my ears from the sounds and screams that exist only in the memory of my abusive past. It feels like HE is right here, punishing me yet again as I scream out in agony...

Feeling hands on my arms I wake up immediately, shoving them off and moving away.

"Baby, you okay? You were screaming and I didn't know what to do.

Trying to clear my head, I glance over to the voice speaking to me. Fuck. Another goddamn nightmare and I'm not alone. Who in the fuck did I bring home from the bar? I let my eyes focus on her hot, tanned body... and I see its Brandy. I needed someone who could go a few rounds with me tonight, thinking I'd be exhausted enough to sleep. Sex, and lots of it, is usually enough to wear me out and keep my nightmares at bay, but that's not the case tonight.

"I think I may have had a bad dream. Can you be a doll and grab me a beer from the kitchen?"

She shakes her head and leaves the room as I head to the bathroom, immediately reaching for the pills Doc prescribed for me when my dreams get out of control.

First it was the sex marathons. They worked for a long time until they didn't. That's when Doc gave me a prescription to help with anxiety and shit. They're working, but I find myself taking more than I'm supposed to.

I came up with an idea that if I use them together, it would be a perfect combination, but now I'm addicted to both. I can't have one without the other, or that's what I tell myself. If only I had popped one before fucking the shit out of Brandy, then sleep would be my friend right now.

After popping a few, I take care of business, washing my hands and rinsing my mouth out with mouthwash. I enter the bedroom just as she walks in with two open beers in her hands. Grabbing one, I gulp down half of it before placing it on the nightstand. Trying to change the mood, I say, "Babe, get your fine ass over here so we can play some more. I feel the need to bury myself in your tight little body."

She takes a sip of her beer, places it on the dresser, and walks toward me, hips swaying provocatively from side to side. That was what got my attention in the first place. This bitch catches your eye with the way she moves her entire body, so seductively.

Brandy has a body that is made for fucking. With her long brown hair, she also has a nice rack with a small waist that widens into a full, perfectly rounded ass. She gives me a sexy as hell smile as she makes her way to me, telling me she's thinking the exact same thing—our fuck session earlier wasn't enough. Brandy loves to fuck. She's not looking for anything beyond sex and she never complains about how kinky it gets, which is perfect for me. I want to fuck her before I have to be back at Wheels & Hogs Garage in the morning, or better yet, in a few hours from now.

I reach for the bottom of the T-shirt she's wearing and remove it, leaving her standing butt-ass naked in front of me. Running my hands down her shoulders, I grab both breasts and squeeze them tightly as she rolls her head back.

"Oh, baby, squeeze harder... pleeease."

I take both nipples between my fingers, rolling and pinching them until they take on a rosy hue. Lowering my head to one, I lick it before placing it between my teeth, and then I bite down.

"Oh my God! Suck them, baby... yes," is what I hear, playing between her two nipples, knowing they are extremely sensitive, I continue to lick, suck, and bite until she starts to lose control, dancing from one foot to the other in anticipation. I can actually smell the arousal from between her thighs, so I start down her body from her breasts, over her soft belly to her pelvic bone. Brandy is shifting her thighs together, trying to relieve the pressure.

Reaching down, I slap both her thighs, causing her to gasp. "I control your orgasm, remember?"

She gives me a slight nod and opens her thighs for me, so I move my hand down to separate her plump lips as she moans. Feeling the moisture on my fingers, I gently move from her pussy lips to the swollen bundle of nerves that I know she's waiting for me to touch. I pull her clit between my fingers and start to rub it, moving it around in circles, soft at first, then harder as her hips start to move in rhythm with my fingers. My other hand is pinching and squeezing her breast, knowing I'm giving her body an overload of sensations.

I stop all together so I can pick her up and lay her on the bed. Bending over her body, I press a firm kiss to her lips and begin licking her lips with my tongue. She moans and sucks on the piercing in my lip while I rub the piercing from my tongue along her top lip. I continue with the pressure on her nipples and her clit, feeling her body tremble and tighten up. Knowing she's close to her orgasm, I plunge my tongue between her full lips, sucking hungrily at her mouth while I move from her clit and shove two fingers into her pussy. She cries out as I pump my fingers in and out, hard and fast, letting my palm hit her clit each time I go in deep. Feeling for her G-spot, I push deeper each time until I hear her whimper. Brandy rocks her hips back and forth, reaching for her orgasm.

Knowing what will push her over the edge, I take my hand from her nipple, lean back on my knees, and reach under her, slipping a finger between her cheeks. With a hard push into her pussy, I put pressure on her asshole at the same time. As each sensation registers, her body reaches overload as her breathing stops for a few brief seconds, then leaves her lips with a loud moan while her walls clamp down on my fingers. I keep pushing as her body continues to tremble until she finally comes down.

My briefs are barely holding my cock inside, so I gently remove my fingers and go to the dresser, grab a condom, and put it on carefully over my pierced cockhead.

"Baby, I'm going to fuck you so hard you'll remember me every time you sit or walk today, and that's a promise."

She giggles, "Bring it on, big man," as she stares at my cock.

I don't waste any time. I grab her by the hips and without hesitation, I plunge myself inside of her, hard and deep. Her head comes off the bed as she gasps from the harsh way I take her, but I don't stop. I'm relentless with her body, pushing her legs out and up over her shoulders, shoving my dick into the hilt while I hold her down, fucking her into the mattress. With each deep thrust, I follow it up with a slight twist of my hips, hitting all of her internal nerve endings.

"Damn, Cadence. I love that big dick of yours and how you work me over with it," she says as she reaches down to rub her clit. "I need to come, baby. Make me come."

When I pull out, she grabs my shaft, giving me a hand job while I fuck her. She wants to come, but she also wants to play so I slow down my pace and let her do what she wants to do. When her hand gets to the thick barbell at the tip, she tugs on it right before I pump back into her. She continues to do this and with every pull on the metal, it sends a jolt through my entire body. I feel my balls start to tighten, knowing it's time.

"Fuck me hard, Cadence. I am so ready to come ooh, just like that..."

Fuck this. I flip her over and pull her ass up and begin fucking her from behind. As I'm slamming into her, I use my thumb to push into her asshole. I move it in and out, keeping rhythm with each thrust into her pussy. I know she's coming the minute I feel her clamp down on my dick like a vise, sucking me back in. Damn this girl. She's got one greedy pussy and I like that shit a lot, but now it's time to concentrate on my own release.

Without any regard for Brandy at all at this point, I begin fucking her so hard that she's practically hanging off the side of the bed. She got hers, now it's time to get mine.

"Fuck, girl, you feel good. Love the way your tight little pussy pulls me in and locks on my cock. That's it, keep doing that shit. Keep tightening your muscles... Holy fuck, Brandy... do not stop doing that!"

I feel that familiar warmth traveling through my

body, causing my balls to tighten up as my cock starts to twitch and I'm there. I feel the warm cum filling up the condom as I slow my thrusts, enjoying the feel of having my wet dick inside of her. Her pussy is still locking on, just having another orgasm of her own. I hold on to the condom, waiting for her to finish.

"Baby, relax your pussy for me."

Brandy takes a deep breath and immediately I feel the release around my cock. Still holding on to the condom, I pull out and give her ass a quick, hard slap.

"Holy shit, Cadence. What the fuck was that for?" I rub my hand over the handprint until her body starts to go soft. When she is totally relaxed, I reach back and slap her other cheek. She screams out, but not in pain. She likes her sex a bit rough, making her a girl after my own heart.

I carefully remove the condom, tie the end, and drop it on the floor then reach for the other condom. Once I'm covered, I step back, smacking each ass cheek a couple of times. Each time her moans are louder and longer as her body reacts to the pain and the pleasure.

"Brandy, get ready. My dick is about to go in your ass."

She shakes her head and pleads for me to do it. Well, what can I say? Baby wants it, then I'm more than happy to give it to her.

That shit was fucking amazing. Turning to face her, I move her sweaty hair off her face, "Honey, anytime you're up for this, you let me know. I haven't blown that hard in a long fucking time." I wait a few minutes to catch my breath before I speak again, "You're more than welcome to stay if you want."

"Are you asking me to stay?" she asks, looking torn.

Not knowing or wanting to know how she feels about the question, I make it easier on her with my next words. No need for this to be awkward. I don't want her to think I'm asking for something I'm not, "Don't bother reading into it. It's an invitation to crash, babe. That's all. We fuck and that's our thing. You wanna leave, that's fine."

For just a moment I saw her actually thinking about staying until I said those words to her. This is all about sex and I have never offered for someone to stick around afterward, but tonight, maybe because of the nightmare, I don't really know if I want her to go, but there is no way I can tell her that. I use her and she uses me. That's how this shit works.

"You do what you want. I've only got a few hours before I got to be at work, so I've gotta clean up and get some shut eye."

I walk into the bathroom and close the door. I can hear her gathering her clothes and getting dressed. It's best that she goes. My nightmares are getting worse, and I don't need her asking questions. She's not someone I would ever share that secret with, only being some chick, I fuck when she's around.

I make a mental note to give that therapist Fern found for me another call. Maybe I do need to talk to a professional again, get some counseling to help me with finding the triggers that are setting these nightmares off again.

After Brandy leaves, I lie in bed knowing sleep won't come. My mind is filled with the horrors that my nightmares bring to the surface. Even though it was years ago, it feels like it happened yesterday. I still use the tools that the therapist gave me to work with when Fern demanded I seek help to get my life back.

Thinking about the triggers that could cause my mind to continuously go back there, I realize with a start what it could be. I've been using meaningless sex as a substitute for real, meaningful relationships. Not saying I don't have good relationships, but most are with the people I work with. I have my mom and two brothers, but because of their pasts they haven't been able to deal with any of it, keeping them from forming any healthy relationships, including with me. We talk a couple of times a year but I can't remember the last time I saw any of them.

I consider Des, Fern, and Doc as my role models, if not also the closest people I have to parental figures. Because of how Des found me, then what Fern, Doc, and Des did for me, it allowed me to open my heart to all three of them. Outside of them, the people I work and hang with are my closest friends. Women come and go because that's how I like it. No relationships, commitments, or expectations; just fucking and lots of it. Although lately it's lost some of its appeal, and that bothers me. I sure as hell don't want to turn into some pussy with feelings and shit.

Grabbing the pills I brought from the bathroom, I pop them in my mouth and take a swig of my now warm beer. Laying my head on the pillow, I hope the pills kick in quickly, shutting my mind off enough to get some much-needed sleep.

CHAPTER TWO

CADENCE

Barely making it through the day without passing out, I decide to join the others at the bar after my dart league kicked major ass, which in my opinion is a cause for celebration. Grabbing a beer from one of the boys, I listen as they shoot the shit about all the usual shit guys talk about at the end of the day. I begin scanning the bar, looking for tonight's piece of ass.

Hearing a familiar laugh, I turn my head in time to see Trinity throw a dart that doesn't even come close to hitting the board. A strange feeling runs through my body as she bends over, holding her stomach while she laughs at herself. As she continues to laugh, I hear her snort through her nose, causing her to move her hands to her face as her girlfriends begin laughing hysterically at her. She's wide-eyed and looking around nervously when her glance falls on me, but then quickly look away.

Grabbing my beer, I head toward Trinity with a feeling of anticipation running through me. I've been having this reaction every time I'm around her for the last couple of months now. The closer I get; my heartbeat increases, and this feeling of excitement overwhelms and surprises me. This is a completely new emotion for me and it bothers me. Not since I arrived in Tranquility have I ever thought of a woman as anything more than a plaything; someone to use as a sexual outlet.

Hearing my name, I'm snapped out of my thoughts only to see Trinity, also walking in my direction with a hesitant smile.

"Hey, Cadence. How did the league do tonight? Sorry I missed it. Work was really busy."

As she stands in front of me, I can't help but notice that she's wearing a long-sleeved shirt in this warm weather, and that her makeup looks darker, like she put too much on. She keeps her face turned a little, but it looks like one eye has a darker coloring than the other. She's purposely keeping distance between us, which seems strange. Something is off, but I'm not going to be the one to bring it up. She looks happy tonight so I'm going to leave it alone.

"Hey, sweetheart. We actually hit the board and won so I'm celebrating," I say, trying to loosen some of the tension I'm feeling. "So what was that you were doing a minute ago? You need some personal lessons on how to shoot darts? If you do, I am always available… for a price."

Tilting her head, she quietly asks, "What's the going rate for a dart instructor?"

"Just a kiss, baby. That's all. You've been holding out on me for months now so you gotta think to yourself, what's one little kiss for the opportunity to get a dart throwing lesson from me?"

Trinity giggles as she turns and walks away from me. She gets to her table, picks up her darts, and returns to my side. "Okay, you've got a deal. One little kiss for a lesson."

I'll take it. I step in back of her, position her behind the line and adjust her stance. Showing her how to hold the dart properly first, I explain to her that it really isn't her whole arm throwing, but her wrist releasing the dart. "Hold it firm but don't crush it. When you go to release, flick your wrist while aiming at the board. Let me show you first."

I grab the dart while pushing her aside so I'm right by the line on the floor. I eyeball the board then release the dart, hitting right off the center. I then turn to Trinity with a shit-eating grin.

~Trinity~

Damn I think to myself. He's so hot. From his broad shoulders down to his narrow waist. What skin you see is covered in tattoos, and he has piercings. There are the ones that are visible, but I've heard the talk about the ones you don't see. As I think about what they could possibly look like, my face starts to get red and that's the moment Cadence turns to stare at me with a wicked grin. "What's the matter, sweetheart? You're all flushed. Did I impress you with my dart throwing skills?"

Taking a minute to memorize the way he looks at me, I shake it off just as quickly, putting my shield back up. "Well, I would hope that you would be somewhat good. You are on a league," I say with a smirk.

We've known each other for a while now, but over the last few months our silly back and forth banter has grown more flirtatious. I'm sure it's nothing to him. He flirts with everyone, giving him the reputation of a manwhore. Some of the tales are epic, but for me, it isn't about that. I genuinely like and enjoy being around him. For some strange reason, I feel like we have a lot in common, but that commonality is something I pray in the deepest part of my heart that I'm wrong about. My life is not at all what I try to make it appear to be to the outside world.

I pull my sleeves down over my hands, drawing Cadence's eyes to me. I pray he doesn't pay enough attention to me to notice the things I've worked so hard on covering up with all this makeup and clothing.

I'm brought back to the present when I feel hands on my hips. I'm so startled that I try to pull away until I look up and see Cadence staring down at my lips. "It's time to pay up, darlin'. You owe me a kiss and I'm calling in on that marker. Don't worry, though. I'll make it as pleasant as possible."

Moving his hands to hold my head in place, he moves his head down until our lips touch. For what seems like forever, but is probably a minute, or even a few seconds, our lips only touch, like he's waiting for something from me. When I'm about to pull away, he pulls me closer to him, never breaking contact between us as he licks the gap between my lips, causing me to gasp and grant him entry.

He takes control of me, tightening his hold on me with one hand and running his other hand to the back of my head, gripping my hair. For a 'little kiss,' this sure has turned into something much more.

He takes his time to taste every part of my mouth, engaging his tongue with mine and I let him. I begin to feel an unfamiliar warmth spread through my body, all the way to my core. I'm so overcome with this feeling that I let my hands wind around his neck as a moan escapes my lips. He deepens the kiss and I feel this untouchable, unattainable man devouring me, just me, and I like it. But as soon as that thought crosses my mind, he releases me, pushing away so abruptly that I have to grasp on to his shirt for balance. Once I can stand properly, I can only think to myself, *that's what he calls a little kiss?*

~Cadence~

I watch her expression as I get my body under control. What the fuck just happened? My dick is so hard I could hammer nails with it. I have to find some release tonight after that shit, it just can't be with Trinity. I didn't mean to take it that far but I didn't expect to react the way I did to her, either. Trinity is a good girl, young and way too naïve. Some of my crude jokes go right over her head, leaving me to explain them to her. By the time I'm done, she still looks lost and the joke's not even funny anymore.

I try being cocky to break the uncomfortable silence between us. "So, what do you think? Did I do a good job of ruining you for any other guy?"

Pulling away from me, she pushes her hair away from her face, trying to look nonchalant but she fails miserably. She's turned on and I know it just by looking at her nipples protruding through her pretty blouse.

"You're okay, Cadence, but I don't have anything to compare it to. I'm sure there are lots of great kissers out there so I wouldn't say you're the best. I know you get plenty of practice though, and you know what they say, 'Practice makes perfect,' so just keep at it. Maybe one day I'll leave this place and come back, just to tell you that I have found the most amazing kisser in the world. If I'm feeling generous, I may give you the chance to prove otherwise."

She giggles as she says this and reaches for her

drink. I can tell she doesn't have a lot of experience, and I find myself wanting to help her out a little bit, but who am I kidding. I just want an excuse to do it again. "Baby, I am all for practicing with you." I can't help myself. I have to kiss her again, so I crush my lips to hers, plundering her mouth mercilessly. The small whimper I receive from her excites me to no end. Fuck, I've got to end this now, even though it's not at all what I want to do, but I can't give her the idea that I want more, even if that's exactly what I want. I won't hurt her feelings.

Breaking off the kiss, I step back, grab my beer, and wink at her as I turn to talk to one of my teammates, dismissing her and feeling shitty about it.

~Trinity~

I'm so confused and frustrated as I'm left standing by myself after Cadence kissed me not once, but twice. He doesn't look affected at all, yet I feel like I'm burning from the inside out. I sit my drink down and run my fingers through my hair. Looking around and not seeing anyone taking an interest in what just happened, including my friends, I make my way toward the restroom. Entering a stall, I prepare to take care of business when I hear the door open and a voice speaks out, "Can you believe he was kissing her? Isn't she like eighteen years old and a virgin? I mean, look at her. She's probably never even given head in her life. There is no way that girl could keep up with his sexual appetite. That man can go all night and do shit to you that will have you begging for him to do it again. I need to go let him know that I'm available because I would love a repeat of last night."

Knowing that voice, I feel sick because it's Brandy, my biggest hater. The pain in my chest makes me feel physically sick. Cadence and Brandy were together last night? I shouldn't be surprised. I had heard rumors of them hooking up, but I've never seen them hang out together.

Why did he just kiss me? Maybe he hadn't seen Brandy yet and was looking for a hookup for the night, but now she's here and available. I know I need to get out of here, even though going home is the last place I want to go. Once I hear the girls leave, I clean up quickly and make my way to the front of the bar. Finding my friends, I give a wave then point to my watch, letting them know I'm heading out.

"Leaving so soon?" Cadence asks as I turn to make my exit. "What's going on? I thought we were having some fun."

Not wanting to give away how hurt and disgusted I am that he spent last night with Brandy, then kissed me here tonight, I pull away from his touch. "I've got an early workday tomorrow, so I've got to get home. Thanks for the dart lesson."

~Cadence~

By her answer I can tell something has upset her, but if I know one thing about Trinity, she keeps shit locked up tight. She isn't going to tell me anything, so I just ask, "We on for karaoke tomorrow?"

She just nods as she leaves through the double doors, not looking back once.

I try to enter the trailer quietly through the back door that leads into the hallway, but I see the light on in the living room. Shit. He's probably awake and waiting for me. Closing the door slowly, I turn to walk down the hall to my room when I hear him yell out my name. My body sags in defeat.

Turning around, I enter the small room and see my dad, Roman, on the couch with a beer in his hand.

"Where have you been, you stupid little bitch? Did I tell you it was okay for you to go out tonight?"

Feeling the tension in my body, I try to calm him down. "I told you that a couple of the girls and I were going to go play darts. Dad, please. It's no big deal."

He rises to his feet and approaches me as I shrink back. Backing me up into a corner, he grabs my arms roughly, twisting them behind my back, which sends immense pain down my arms because they are already bruised from the abuse the night before. Knowing what is coming, I go to my safe place, and all I can see is Cadence kissing me.

That image plays over and over in my mind as I receive punch after punch on my already beaten body.

CHAPTER THREE

CADENCE

When I wake up, the first thing I think about is the scene at the bar last night. I know I shouldn't have taken it that far with Trinity, that wasn't the plan. I always have fun with her, but damn, for a girl who says she's not very experienced, she can fucking kiss. I don't know what I was expecting to happen throughout the night after that, but I didn't expect her to turn cold and leave so abruptly.

Once she was gone, I proceeded to have one too many beers and took Brandy in the bathroom for a quick blowjob. Trinity left me all hot and bothered, but Brandy took care of it. Funny thing about it was, watching Brandy suck me off wasn't really working for me but as soon as I started thinking of that beautiful golden hair and that hot as hell kiss, I came hard and fast. After I blew my load, I couldn't get away from Brandy fast enough.

Trinity is so different from all the other women in

my life. Really, the only thing I do know about her is that she's not easy or slutty. A girl of twenty-two, with little experience is refreshing. Sex is never a problem for me because women throw themselves at me, making it too easy. Trinity has started to become a challenge in my mind because we started out friends and have been ever since. No sex to muck things up, but maybe it's that connection we've made that has caused me to see her in a whole different light. Our relationship has never been based on sex, making it easy and simple, but most of all, important.

Thinking back on the first time I met her; I was in town picking up lunch for the crew at Wheels & Hogs while she was walking out of the deli. With the sun reflecting off her golden hair, she looked ethereal. Her skin was flawless and her figure slim and round in all the right places. The sight of her gave me an instant hard-on. When I walked toward her, she immediately put her eyes down but I caught her checking me out too. I found myself stopping her, not ready to let her walk away. I introduced myself and from that moment we just clicked. I asked her to meet me at the local bar that night for karaoke and she said she would come if I didn't mind her bringing a friend. It was from there that our friendship began and continued to grow.

As time went on, I got to know her and found out what a goofball she was. The more time I spent with her, it was apparent that she was someone special. She was one of the few people who could make me laugh and made me comfortable enough to be myself. I've always felt like we had a lot in common, that she understood things about me even though I had never said a word. Maybe I pushed something last night that she wasn't ready for. Maybe she saw something I didn't; that our friendship would never be the same if we crossed that line.

Reaching for my phone, I send her an instant message, just to check on her. Holding the phone in my hand, I wait for her response. After five minutes of silence, I put it down on the bed and go take care of business. Having to get ready for work, I shower and get dressed. Going into the kitchen to put on the coffee, I hear my phone alert, so I grab it to check the message.

Hey, Cadence. Thanks for checking on me. Not feeling too good so in bed getting some rest. Probably not gonna make it to the bar tonight so can I get a rain check?"

No problem, baby. Feel better.

I throw the phone on the counter and proceed to get ready for a long day at the shop.

~Trinity~

I can't get out of bed because I'm in so much pain. Dad really pushed the limits and I've been out of my mind with pain ever since. I'm having trouble breathing, guessing I have a cracked rib or two. I attempt to take as deep of a breath as I possibly can, without screaming, to try and calm my thoughts.

Trying not to focus on the pain, I replay last night with Cadence over and over in my mind. Even with everything that happened after I came home; the thought of Cadence gives me a small bit of peace. The way he kissed me made me feel beautiful and desirable, in the right way, for the first time in my life. Even before last night, our friendship has shown this connection between us, and I don't have a clue why; we're total opposites. I'm quiet, shy, and reserved—never drawing attention to myself—always hiding in the background. Cadence, on the other hand, is blunt and in your face. Sex just pours off him, drawing women to him like he's a drug and he's their fix. I see it every time I'm with him. Women's eyes follow his every move, not even caring if I'm sitting with him or not. They have no shame when it comes to getting his attention.

The thing that drew me to him was the sweet way he treated me, never making moves on me, or trying to make me another notch on his belt. He's always treated me with respect and that has meant so much to me, but things have been changing, or evolving would be a better term, between us lately. I see him looking at me differently and I'm doing the same with him. Last week he asked me to slow dance and it was the first real contact we've had between us. I've watched him so I know that he's a really good dancer, but I wasn't ready for this type of dance with him. He held me close, making me lose myself in the feel of his body against mine. His hands began moving along my waist, slowly to my hips where he began to pull me into him. I could feel his excitement as he ground his hips against me, telling me he was feeling exactly what I was feeling. Not knowing what to do, I tried to pull away, only to have Cadence pull me in even closer. I wasn't ready for it. I never wanted to even think of a sexual relationship with anyone.

Thankfully the song ended, and I walked away and decided then to stay away for a while. It was just a dance, but it was so much more than that. I knew I couldn't let him get too close because I never wanted him to find out my dirty secret.

CHAPTER FOUR

CADENCE

I watch as Trinity enters the bar with a couple of her coworkers and I notice immediately that she looks pale, almost sickly. She also looks a lot thinner than the last time I saw her. Her color is off and even in the dark, I can see the fading bruises on her neck and face under the heavy makeup she wears to cover them up. What the fuck is going on and who would beat such a sweet girl? Not wanting to scare her off, I just smile and wave. Besides her appearance, I can't believe how relieved I feel to finally see her. The last few weeks we've been texting, even talking on the phone a time or two, but this is the first time I'm actually seeing her since I kissed her.

I keep my distance from her most of the night, not wanting to crowd her, but I can feel her eyes on me whenever she thinks I'm not paying attention. Having her so close, knowing she's watching me makes me hard as fuck. What the hell is wrong with me? Shit. Not what I need right now, especially as Trinity starts to walk toward me.

Pulling a chair from an empty table, I sit my ass down just as she stops in front of me. "Hey, Cadence. How are you?"

Looking closely at her, I reply harshly, "Who the hell has been using you for a punching bag, Trinity? Better yet, why haven't you called me for help? You look like shit."

She immediately turns to leave as I hear a soft sob coming from her as both of her hands go to cover her face. I reach for her shoulders and as soon as I touch her, a cry escapes her lips. Stepping back, I walk around to face her, moving her hands from her face and pulling her into me.

"What's going on, baby? Please talk to me so I can help you."

"I can't tell you. I can't tell anyone so please pretend, for me, that nothing is wrong. It would be horrible if anyone ever found out, including you, so please, Cadence, for me, just let it go. Spending time with you always makes my nights a little brighter, so let's have some fun, okay?"

Taking in a deep breath, I look at the woman in front of me and know I need to find out what is going on in her life and where this abuse is coming from. I know if I try to push her into telling me, I could lose the only friend outside the garage I've made, so grabbing her gently by the elbow, I pull her to the dance floor as a slow ballad starts to play. I align our bodies and pull her head to rest just above even with my shoulder holding her close as we sway to the music, content to hold each other with no questions asked, at least for now.

As the night goes on, I begin asking questions; simple, easy questions I hope won't make her think that I'm being intrusive, but I need to figure out what the hell is going on with her. She obviously feels she has no one to turn to, so if I can't get the answers I need from her, I have to find some way to protect her.

The evening passes with no real answers, but since it's getting closer to closing time I decide to give her what she asked for—some fun. I drag her back out to the dance floor, hoping to bring out that beautiful smile of hers and it works. We dance slowly to every song played, laughing, and enjoying each other's company. There is definitely a sexual undercurrent, which is becoming harder to deny between us, and I don't know if it's something I want to fight anymore. We dance and laugh the rest of the night, staying until it's time for the bar to close.

"Can I give you ride home?" I ask her.

Shaking her head, she points to a car waiting with the door open. "No thanks. I have a ride but I really want to thank you for tonight, Cadence. I really had a lot of fun and I like how your reputation doesn't get in the way of our friendship."

"What reputation are you talking about?"

Shifting from one foot to the other with her head down, she shrugs her shoulders. I reach and tilt her chin up so I can look into her eyes as I move closer to her. "Tell me what you've heard about me, sweetheart."

Clearing her throat, she stares straight into my eyes and bluntly says, "You're a manwhore." Her body goes stiff, and she looks shocked. "Oh my gosh! I am so sorry. I didn't mean for it to come out like that, I swear. Sometimes my brain and mouth don't run on the same channels, but the rumors are that you will screw anything that walks, talks, and breathes."

Fuck, if she only knew, I think to myself.

~Trinity~

I hate when things just spill out of my mouth like word vomit. I'm an idiot. I expect him to get mad but what I don't expect is for him to throw his head back and roar with laughter.

He grabs me close, still laughing as he leans in and whispers, "Trinity. Any time you want to see if those rumors are true, you just let me know, okay?"

Taking my face in both his hands, he lightly kisses my lips. Standing perfectly still, I'm not sure what to do so I just stand there and let him take the lead. Once I open my lips to kiss him back, he really starts to kiss me, devouring my mouth. I whimper as heat starts to spread through my body. With just a kiss, I want him to take anything he wants from me.

Getting lost in the moment, I press my body into his, feeling his muscles tense under my hands. At the same time, he grabs my hips, shoving his erection against my stomach, causing me to gasp into his mouth and reach up to grasp his shoulders tightly.

Although we're in a dark area on the side of the building, he steers me closer to the wall, where it's even darker. We continue to make out like a couple of teenagers, both of us grinding into one another, breathing heavily into one another's mouth. "Come home with me tonight. I want you so fucking bad, Trinity."

He grabs my hand and pushes it down the front of his jeans, where I wrap my hand around his hard, thick length with all of his piercings and watch him grind his teeth in pleasure. I grip him tighter as he begins thrusting himself into my hand, bringing his head back down to mine for a toe-curling kiss.

In a rush, my mind comes back to me and I'm humiliated by what I'm about to let happen. I'm not ready for this kind of intimacy, and I'm ashamed of myself for letting it get this far. I feel like a tease, but regardless of how this is going to make me look to him, I gently remove my hand and place it on his chest, pushing him away. "Cadence, I can't do this. Please move back because I have to go. I'm so sorry."

~Cadence~

Disbelievingly, I look down into her eyes and see fear. This shit is like a cold bucket of water thrown on me and I instantly move back. Running my hands through my hair, I manage to take a long draw of air into my lungs, trying to get my body and mind back under control.

After a few moments I speak to Trinity carefully, "What's going on, babe? This is the second time you've shut me down when I made a move. First, it was the kiss at the bar and now tonight. We're both adults, so what's the harm in having some fun? Don't you want me?" I give her a second to process, but when she doesn't say a word, I continue, "We've been hanging out for months now and I have never once pressured you or treated you with anything but respect, but what the hell is this? If friendship is what you're looking for, that's cool. No problem. If you want to be friends with benefits, we can do that too, but you can't let me think one thing then do another. Just talk to me and tell me what you want, and I'll do it."

"Answer one question for me before I answer yours. Since the night you kissed me, we've been talking more and you've given me the impression that you're feeling something more between us than friendship, so I have to ask; have you slept with anyone since the first time you kissed me?"

I don't respond, but I know the look on my face is one of guilt, which gives her the answer she is seeking.

"This is why I can't, Cadence. I've thought about what the difference is between all the girls you take home every night and me. I know it's because they haven't given you a challenge, but I have. They don't mind sleeping with you within minutes of meeting you, but I've never given you the impression that I would, making me something you haven't had. Sex should mean something, not just an act you do when the mood hits you. I'm sorry, but I won't be one of those girls. Everything I've heard about you is true."

"You know what, little girl? Maybe you're right. You were a challenge, but I don't need this bullshit for a piece of ass, no matter how fine. I don't chase it; it comes to me. Have a great night." I turn and walk away, leaving Trinity to think on that.

~Trinity~

After I hear Cadence squeal out of the parking lot, I walk around the corner to my friend's car, trying to keep my emotions from ripping me in half. He doesn't know what my life is like or what I have to endure, so how could he ever understand my way of thinking? Sex is sex to him. It doesn't matter to him who it's with or where it's at, just as long as he gets it when he wants it.

As my friends chat about things of no importance, I sit in the back seat, thinking that I made the right decision to stop this when I did. I don't need or want to be someone's fuck buddy, booty call, or whatever it is he wants to use me for. I don't need something else to break me emotionally or physically. I have enough of that in my life and I'm not looking for more of it from someone else. Too bad Cadence turned out to be exactly what I don't need.

Hearing my phone beep, I pull it out of my pocket and see that it's an IM from Cadence. I really want to ignore it in case he wants to make me feel shittier about tonight, but I put on my big girl panties and open the message.

Cadence: I am so sorry for being a total jerk no asshole. Didn't mean to pressure you into anything, just got carried away. We have a great friendship, and I can't lose you. Please give me a chance to fix this.

Me: Then treat me with the same respect you would as a friend. I won't allow you to treat me like shit because I tell you what I feel. Tonight, was not ok, but I'm willing to move past this. I'll talk to you soon.

. . .

Waiting to see if he replies, the girls drop me at the corner a few blocks away from the entrance of the trailer park where I always ask to be dropped. Making my way to the trailer, I open the door and I'm so relieved to see that I'm alone. Going to my room, I shut the door and start to change into my pj's when I hear the bing on my phone. Looking at the message, I smile to myself before reading the entire message.

Cadence: I won't let you down. I want to see where this thing between us could go, so no more girls, just us. Sleep well. I'll see you soon."

CHAPTER FIVE

DES

Across town, after spending a couple of hours on the computer getting all the files organized with the emails printed together, I decide I need more coffee. Heading to the kitchen, I see the coffee pot shut off automatically, so I pour some in my cup and put it in the microwave to warm it up. As I'm getting it ready, I hear a bike coming up to the front of the house. I grab my cup and head toward the door where I can already see Doc walking up through the glass in the door, looking defeated. Shit. Something must be wrong for Doc to come all the way out here. Please God, don't let it be Fern.

I open the door and Doc just about falls into the hallway. I grab his shoulders, asking him if he's okay when he looks up at me, eyes and face wet with tears. I gently lead him to the family room and down into a chair. Doc just leans his elbows on his knees, placing his face in his hands. I lean down and ask him, "What the fuck? You're scaring the shit out of me so tell me what's up, man."

Doc raises his head and says softly, "Des, I can't take much more. I had to get out of there; needed a break, man. My wife is wasting away while I have to sit and watch, twiddling my thumbs, not able to do a fucking thing to help."

I put my hand on Doc's shoulder. "Do you want some coffee, or something stronger?"

"Coffee would be great. Thanks, just black," Doc replies. I walk through to the kitchen and dump what is in the pot.

"Give me a minute, Doc. Gonna make a fresh pot."

Once the coffee is brewing, I open the fridge and realize all I have is leftover pizza from last night. I take it out and throw it on a plate, then into the microwave. After pouring a cup of black coffee, I grab that and two pieces of pizza, taking it to Doc. "I know it isn't much, but here's your coffee and a couple slices of leftover pizza. You look like you could eat something." I grab my coffee and sit on the sofa, watching Doc devour the pizza. Getting back up, I get the last two pieces and offer him what's left. He grabs one and leaves the other one for me and we eat in silence.

Doc finally looks at me and pours his heart out, "I am so fucking lost, Des. I don't know what to do. We're about to lose our home; just found out they started foreclosure proceedings. On top of that, the hospital bills keep growing and even with your insurance from the shop, we are so far in debt I don't think we can ever pay this shit off. Fern is trying to make adjustments to her treatments and in-patient stays. Doctors are against all of her attempts. With her weakened state, she needs to have constant care at all times from professionals since she's going through experimental procedures." He scrubs his face with his hands and continues, "If this treatment doesn't work out, I don't think that I will be able to go on, man. Fern is my heart, my soul, and my life. We have been together since high school. All of our dreams have been shot to hell with her cancer. What can I do, Des? At this moment, I am so damn lost."

I take a deep breath, seeing now is the time to tell Doc what I've been working on, but I have to do it in a way that he doesn't think its charity because, otherwise, he won't accept it.

"Doc, I have something to tell you. It's something I have been working on for a while now, so hear me out. What do you think of a charity ride for Fern? It would include the Bone Marrow Registry and getting donations, looking for a match for her, but also building up the resources for the organization."

Doc looks confused. "What the hell are you talking about, Des?" I get up and go to the office to grab all the folders off my desk, returning to the sofa with my hands full.

Placing them on the table, I tell Doc, "Take a minute and look at what I have so far. This isn't just an idea, Doc. I have a lot of time invested in this."

Doc grabs a file and starts to look through it.

Shocked at what he finds, he grabs another, and then another, looking through each and every one. When he's finally finished, he looks at me, eyes full of tears that he is desperately trying to hold back. "Oh my God, Des. What the fuck have you been up to, and why?"

I take a moment before I reply, "Doc, I know what it feels like to lose your world. When my parents were killed, it changed the entire direction of my life. I have always admired, and even envied at times, your relationship with Fern. You two define what is to be a couple, a team that's in a relationship and still madly in love. Shit, everyone can see it and have experienced your love in one way or another. When your clinic was up and running, the way you two worked together for the best interest of the less fortunate was simply humbling. Since Fern started her fight with cancer, not once have you asked me for special privileges because of her sickness. You show up for your scheduled hours and do the work with no complaints. I can't image the pressure you feel all day, every day, but I want to help in any way that I can. In the next day or so, I will be bringing this to the crew at Wheels and Hogs. You know, better known as our fucked-up extended family." We both bark out a short laugh. "I need help, and with the shop's help, including the kids, we will be able to get this going a lot quicker than me trying to do this alone."

This time when Doc looks at me, he's not even trying to hold back the tears. "Desmond, I have no words that could even come close to expressing how much this means to me. No one has ever done anything like this for me in my entire life. To know that you care that much about my Fern fills my heart with hope. What are your plans, and do you want me to tell Fern about this? Knowing my wife, as we both do, she'll be overcome with your show of love and support."

I shake my head. "First let me talk to the Horde, and then you can bring Fern in if she's up to it. Everyone would love to see her."

We continue our conversation, looking over all that has been accomplished already, taking a few hours to do so. Doc gets up and heads to the door. He turns and grabs me, pulling me in for a man hug, telling me, "Thank you isn't enough, but that's all I have."

"Don't thank me, dude. Let's see what we can come up with." This gets a small laugh out of Doc. "You okay to drive, Doc?"

He nods his head as he moves through the front door. "I've got to get back to Fern. I'm feeling hopeful all of a sudden and I need to hug and tell her how much I love her. I'll see you at the shop, Des."

My thoughts go to all the changes I see in the near future. Between this endeavor to help Doc and Fern, there is my concern about Cadence's current path in life, or lack thereof. Something is bothering him, and I have no idea what it could be. He has this constant look of worry and confusion, which with this kid never leads to anywhere good.

On top of all of that, I'm worried about the obvious crush Willow has for Wolf, who seems to be blind to the entire situation. I know a little bit about Wolf and from what I know, this combination just spells disaster. Sooner or later, Willow will make her feelings known for Wolf and that will become an issue in the shop. Not to mention all the other employees with their issues, secrets, and just their lives in general.

After Doc leaves, I put all of the files back in the office. In a few more weeks, I'll get this charity ride ready to bring to the table. It's time to get everyone on board.

CHAPTER SIX

TRINITY

I look at my reflection in the mirror, smiling. All my hard work paid off. My hair is curled at the ends, shining down my back. The light makeup I applied makes my eyes stand out, and the gloss on my lips makes them look fuller. The dress I'm wearing is borrowed from one of my coworkers. It's a deep purple wrap dress. It accents my figure while leaving something to the imagination. The V-neck shows a bit of cleavage, and the hem is a couple of inches above the knee. I have on a pair of silver pumps that match my jewelry.

Tonight, is going to be special; I can feel it. Cadence asked me to go to dinner and then out for a drive. I know what that means. I'm both anxious and nervous, but I can't deny that Cadence is everything I would want in a man. Attractive, funny, quick-witted, and always up for anything. We have done some really fun stuff over the last couple of weeks like paint balling, bumper cars, the movies, and not to mention, dancing and karaoke.

The more time we spend together, the deeper my feelings grow. We have these amazing and intense make-out sessions that have led to some interesting moments for me, since this is all so new to me. My body starts to heat up just thinking about some of things we've done together, like the night we were at his apartment and the making out turned into a groping session. His huge hands covered and played with my breasts, which drove me wild. Then there was the time he unzipped his jeans, pulled out his pierced cock and showed me how he likes to be touched. That night I was enthralled with that part of his body; how hard but smooth it was, and how it felt different in my hand from before. He showed me how to move my hand up and down hard, but not too hard, and then I remember feeling him get thicker as he released. I was fascinated as I watched it spurt out onto his stomach and my hand.

I push my hair out of my face, feeling a little light-headed and a bit wet between my legs. I'm amazed at finding and learning what my body likes with Cadence. He's slowly showing me what it feels like to be touched the right way, kissed the right way, and handled in the right way. I understand now what you're supposed to feel when you are with someone you choose and want to be with. I'm also starting to understand my own sexuality, even going as far as masturbating a couple of times and remembering how Cadence did it. It doesn't feel the same, but it allows me to figure out what I like and don't like.

He has never pushed me since that episode about a month ago on the side of the bar. He's being patient with me, letting me find my own pace, and going with the flow. When we had gotten close, he told me that it was my choice. I was still scared to death about taking that last step, but I was also really worked up. When he put his hand down my pants for the first time, I lost it. Never having a man touch me like that, I had no idea what to expect and I came instantly. So, when his fingers put pressure on my clit, I began to thrash around, not being able to control what my body was feeling. This happened a few more times after that, when he never said anything, but always looked at me strangely until finally one night, he asked, "What's the matter, baby?"

"I don't know. It feels so... ticklish at first, but then it's so intense. I can't stop myself."

"Trinity, have you ever had someone touch you like this? Are you a virgin?"

I immediately got upset but I sucked it up and only said, "I have been touched before, but never like you touch me. You make me want to enjoy it." After that, I didn't fight the feelings as his fingers not only played with my clit, but he began to slowly put one, then two fingers inside of me and the feeling was amazing. He knew exactly what to do and a pressure built inside of me until I fell apart under his hands. I was becoming a huge fan of orgasms.

Knowing my time is limited, I grab my purse and head out of the trailer, thankful my dad is again at the bar. Walking to the entrance of the trailer park and making my way a few streets down, I wait for my cab. I don't want Cadence to see where I live so I'm meeting him in town at the restaurant he picked. I'm so excited because this is actually my very first date.

Arriving before Cadence, I wait outside the restaurant, sitting on one of the benches watching as people go by. As I look at the crowds, a voice to my left makes me look in that direction, "Wow. Look at Little Miss Innocent all dressed up and all alone..."

Raising my eyes, I see Brandy and her mean girl clique. Deciding to ignore them, I look away, but this doesn't deter Brandy from pressing on, "I hope you're enjoying your time with Cadence because in no time at all, he'll get bored and I'll be on his cock and in his bed. It's real comfortable place to fuck, that's for sure. You do get what I'm saying, don't you, little girl? To be clear, I have fucked, and sucked in every position you can think of with Cadence, and I will again. He loves pussy and he loves women, so don't think you're something special and he's going to be your knight in shining armor."

A loud growl comes from behind me and before I can turn around, Cadence is in front of me, facing off with Brandy and her friends. "You truly are a jealous bitch! You keep your filth away from Trinity and don't you ever talk to her like that again, do you hear me? You will never be back in my bed, I can promise you that, so all of you get the hell away from us—I said get the fuck away NOW!"

By the end of Cadence's rant, I'm shaking, and tears are building up in my eyes as I struggle to hold them back. Feeling Cadence sit next to me, he pulls me into his side. "Baby, are you okay? Please don't listen to that spiteful bitch." He drops his head to my forehead. "You knew I had a past, but I promised you I wouldn't sleep with anyone else if we were making a go of this, and I meant it, okay? Please don't let the past get in the way of what we are trying to have right now."

Trying to get myself together I realize that Cadence is right, so I grab his hand and smile. "I'm starving, so let's go eat."

Cadence helps me to my feet, whistling as he takes in my outfit. "Damn, girl. You are one beautiful woman."

We go off laughing together as we head into the restaurant.

This evening has been the best night of my life. We sat in the fancy restaurant talking, laughing, and just being together. The food was amazing and Cadence ordered a bottle of wine to go with our food, which was excellent. We shared stories of our lives, nothing deep or meaningful, as we both have secrets we aren't ready to share, but we did talk about things like what we liked to do and what we would love to do. Our conversation ran smoothly and effortlessly, as did the wine. I was feeling so good that when dinner ended and he suggested we go back to his place, I said yes. Maybe tonight would be the night.

When we arrive at his apartment, it being above Wheels & Hogs where he works, I feel the change between us immediately. I try to remain calm because I know now I can trust Cadence. He approaches me slowly, reaching for me and walking me to the couch. He lightly kisses my forehead and looks into my eyes as he asks, "Baby, are you okay? You know I won't do anything you don't want to do."

Shaking my head, the alcohol gives me the liquid courage I need because I lean forward and start to kiss him. He responds immediately, kissing me back just as passionately, while moving his hands to the front of my wrap dress to squeeze my breasts as I push into his hands. Moaning into his mouth, I start to run my hands down his chest, feeling all the muscles that lead to the six-pack narrowing to his V.

Neither one of us feel the need to take our time as Cadence pushes the top of my dress off my shoulders, laying me back onto the couch and lowering his head to lick at my nipples through my pretty black and purple bra. He tugs the bra down, pulling my breast up and over the cup, and he begins to suck, bite, and lick until I begin whimpering loudly, but he doesn't stop. He's obviously figured out what a turn-on it is for me when he does this to my breasts. He continues to squeeze them while sucking as much as he can into his mouth while simultaneously licking my nipple. At this point, I'm screaming with need.

Knowing exactly what to do to me, he reaches lower and moves his hand under my dress, pushing past my panties to run his fingers over my clit. He starts to rub it in circles, then to my complete shock, he grabs it between his fingers and pinches it until my hips start to pump up into his hand. He stops and inserts two fingers into my wetness and begins to thrust into me. I feel my walls grasping his fingers each time he goes to pull them out. I'm starting to lose it when he puts pressure on a spot that has me feeling like I'm peeing on myself, which I'm not, but it's the most amazing feeling. I'm shamelessly pumping my pussy against his fingers, begging him to keep doing what he's doing when I feel something running down my ass cheeks.

"What was that Cadence? That was... it was—

"It was an orgasm, baby. It's the most intense orgasm a woman can have." He then lifts his fingers from my body and slowly brings them to his mouth. He proceeds to clean my orgasm from his fingers and hand, never taking his eyes from me while he does this. "You taste so fucking sweet, Trinity." As I start to blush, he reaches for my face. "Never be embarrassed, sweetheart. You have nothing to worry about. This is all normal, and I'm truly enjoying this as you make me so fucking hard, baby."

Feeling shy and unsure, but still going with the liquid courage running through my body, I reach for the button of his jeans. Undoing the button, I unzip his zipper, all the while, running the back of my hand along his hard length. Reaching inside of his briefs, I take a firm grip of his cock, pumping my hand once down his pierced shaft, watching his eyes roll back as he relaxes, moving off me and onto his side.

"Shit, Trinity. I could blow in your hand right now, baby. Pump harder." Instead, I remove my hand and stand up. I watch as his look of confusion changes as I begin undressing myself in front of him. Once I'm completely naked, he looks at me as if I'm the most beautiful thing he has ever seen.

Jumping up from the couch, he lifts me over his shoulder, taking me to the bedroom, and none too gently, throws me on the bed. I watch as he begins removing his clothes, this time standing before me with the body of a Greek god. He reaches over to his dresser to pull out a condom and once he takes it out of its packaging, I watch him as he slowly slides it over his pierced cock, and I begin to feel scared and excited. He must see it because he makes sure that it's on securely and maneuvers me on the bed so he's between my legs, on his knees, looking down at me. Neither one of us says a word as he grabs his cock in his hand and begins moving up and down his shaft, smiling at me as I watch him. It is the sexiest thing I have ever seen in my life, and I know there is no going back after this, and I'm okay with that.

He starts to glide the head of his cock along my clit, causing me to jump but he holds me down with his other hand until he's positioned at my entrance. He moves the head in slowly, watching my reaction. When I raise my hips higher, urging him to go farther, he shoves in deep and I push into him, needing to finally feel his cock inside of me.

"I swear, Trinity. I'm gonna fuck you and give you a night that you will never forget. That's a fucking promise"

I'm counting on it.

He's a fucking madman. He blows my mind with the things he makes my body feel and do. He's put me into positions I never thought were possible and giving me so many orgasms that I lost track.

We've been at this all night and there are four condoms on the floor. I never imagined someone could have so much sex in a short amount of time, but I have no complaints. He's a machine. I'm ruined. I could do this with him every day for the rest of my life. The piercings are just the icing on the cake.

Once we finally catch our breaths and come down from our acrobatics act, he pulls me in close and cuddles with me. *This is heaven*, I think to myself as a tear slides down my cheek.

∼Cadence∼

Even with everything we've done tonight, I know that somehow, someway, I'm going to mess this up. I always do. I'm nothing but a fuckup and Trinity deserves so much better, but I'm a selfish prick and just couldn't stay away from her. I can only hope that everything will work out in the long run.

Feeling her relax against me, I hold on to her tightly, afraid that I'm going to lose her. I'm going to lose this feeling and never find the peace I always beg God for. I'm going to fuck up, and I will never get that peace because I don't deserve it.

CHAPTER SEVEN

DES

As I park my 2010 smoky gray Camaro, I take a sip of coffee and run my hand through my hair. Glancing at my lifelong ambition with a critical eye, I see nothing out of the ordinary.

There are lots of windows across the front, so I can see people moving around and intermingling. Willows' flowerbeds are in full bloom, making the front of the shop look professional, with a soft, personal touch. The six overhead doors are either partially or fully opened and I can hear the music coming out from the shop. Guys are already jamming as they work, moving back and forth from their toolboxes to the cars or bikes they are currently working on. It always amazes me how efficiently the shop runs, almost by itself, because I know in my heart that it's the people I have closest that keep it running like a fine-oiled machine. Shutting my car down, I head to the front door.

Walking through the doors of the shop, I see Wolf

look up at me from behind the counter, giving me a chin lift.

"Where the hell is Cadence? I didn't see him in the garage. He has that big job today and he told me that he would start early."

Wolf just lifts his shoulders, not giving me an answer.

After last night's events of breaking things off with Katie, I'm not in the best of moods. Knowing all the work that needs to be done today, I'm not happy with Cadence for blowing off work when he promised to handle his shit. He continues to prove to me that no matter how good he is, he's not getting any closer to being responsible, which has me thinking twice about why I'm still letting him work here.

Once I get to my office door, I go to turn the knob when I hear soft mumbling, followed by a woman moaning. I know what I'll find when I open the door; it wouldn't be the first time I'd walked in on one of the boys getting busy in my office. Dammit! Don't these guys have a place other than my office? I want to storm in and raise hell with whoever is in there, but I stop myself. There is a female in there too, and I don't have it in me to embarrass a woman, no matter how pissed off I am. I stand and wait, trying to focus my rage on something else, which is not possible. I'm getting more pissed by the second when I hear, of all assholes, Cadence yell out, "FUCK!" I know by his tone that something is wrong.

I charge into my office to see the manwhore who

has no boundaries. He's not even totally naked, just has his jeans and briefs hanging down to his ankles. I try not to look but there is a naked, busty blonde scrambling off my desk, shrieking and grabbing for her clothes to hide herself. I guess I should have knocked first, but I thought something was wrong.

As she's having a nervous breakdown, I look over at Cadence, who is looking down at the condom still on his dick. I look down to see what it is that has him looking so freaked out and see that his piercing has gone completely through the condom.

"Baby, please tell me you're clean and on the pill," Cadence asks his friend.

She stops and gawks at Cadence. Through her tears of embarrassment, she replies, "Yes, Cadence, I'm clean, and no, I'm not on the pill. Why? Where the hell did that come from?"

Cadence shakes his head and starts to dress. "This is my boss and I need to get back out there. Thanks for stopping by, I love a good fuck in the middle of the day, babe, but you gotta go now.

The young girl's eyes fill with even more tears as he goes about getting dressed and dismissing her. She says to him in a soft, broken voice, "Is this all this was for you? Are you telling me that I'm nothing more than a 'Brandy' to you? Do you know me at all, Cadence Powers?" At this, Cadence laughs nervously, looking repeatedly at me standing in the doorway.

"Baby, you said you heard about me before we started this and you know how I'm all about having fun and getting laid. If you're ever up for it, I wouldn't mind going at it again with you." Cadence then buttons up his jeans with shaking hands, avoiding the young girl's stare as he passes by me with his head down.

~Cadence~

Once I pass Des, I feel my entire body start to shut down emotionally. What the fuck did I just do? What the fuck did I just say? I'm in a fucking fog as I make my way to the bathroom to clean up. None of this was meant to happen, but she's right. My God, that's exactly how I treated her after fucking her on my boss's desk like some bar bitch... just like a "Brandy."

She showed up early for me to take a look at her car. She followed me to Des's office to find some paperwork. We were joking and laughing, then I kissed her and it led to this.

I freaked out at seeing the rip in the condom, then Des walked in and I started being a dick, trying to get out of there before anyone caught on as to what just happened. I fucked up big time. I panicked and now I have to fix this shit with her.

~Des~

I feel the anger starting in my chest and glare at the naked girl on my desk. I want her gone. I don't have time for this shit today; too much to do and I'm already behind schedule. I also know that I'm gonna have words with all the guys because this shit is not going to happen again.

They can't keep acting like they're teenagers anymore, except for Jagger, that is, Dee's son. They all have responsibilities that need looking after and this shit has to stop. This is work, their place of employment, not a damn brothel.

"You gonna sit on my desk all day, darlin', or are you waiting for one of my other boys to come in and get a taste?"

I know I'm being a bastard right now and I know I should care about what was just done to her by Cadence, but I don't. Right now my head feels like it is going to blow the fuck off my shoulders from my night of drinking and my own female drama. I can't take much more, even though I just got here. I'm ready for this day to be over.

She makes an attempt to get off my desk and starts to dress when her shoulders begin to shake uncontrollably as she starts to cry even harder. Damn Cadence to hell and back for leaving me, yet again, to do his dirty work. I reach in my back pocket for my bandana and hand it to her.

She lifts her head to me to say, "I can't apologize enough for this, sir. Cadence and I have been seeing each other for a while now, and this wasn't why I was here today. I'm also real sorry for crying. I have no idea why he would treat me this way. Everything has been going so great between us. I saw him looking at his condom so I know what happened, but I can't believe how he treated me just now. I just really need to get out of here.

"Honey, if you know how he is, why would you put yourself in this position? He's a player; always has been. I don't see that changing anytime soon. Let's finish getting you dressed and out of here, so you don't have to deal with him. What's your name?"

"Trinity Vinkers."

I take her hand and look her in the eyes, stating firmly, but gently, "Trinity, learn a lesson here today. Take your time when it comes to men. Don't let anyone pressure you and don't let yourself feel pressured to do anything you don't want to do. I hope to God that this accident doesn't become a pregnancy, but if you find out that you are pregnant, here is my card. I want you to call me. I will help you as much as I can with whatever you decide to do, I can promise you that. I'm not going to sugarcoat this so I will be very honest with you, okay? We both know what caused him to say those things and run out of here like a little pussy, so do not expect to count on Cadence being around if you find out you are pregnant. He's not that guy, as much as I wish he was but, darlin', don't let him ruin you. Become a strong, independent woman who doesn't need or depend on any man. Respect yourself enough to know when you are being played. You seem like a nice kid, and I don't want to see you any more hurt than you already are." Trinity's head shoots up to look at me gently smiling down on her with a slight smile.

She wipes her eyes and nose in the bandana and straightens her shoulders, giving me a nod. I turn as she finishes getting dressed then I walk her not only out of my office, but also past the guys in the shop, including Cadence, who is acting like he doesn't even know the girl he fucked and left minutes before.

Trinity pulls away from me, asking for a second and walks over to Cadence who is talking to Archie. As she nears the two, Cadence turns around just as Trinity reaches him. I watch as they just stare at one another. She obviously wants him to see what he has just done to her, and I can't blame her. Shit, I'm hoping she punches him at this point, but after what seems like forever, she reaches out to touch his cheek softly. Everyone in the shop is watching and trying to get closer as they see Trinity lean in toward Cadence.

"Cadence, you will never know how this one mistake will change everything for me, for the both of us. You asked me to trust you and I did. That was a first for me and I don't think you understand what it took for me to do that with everything that has happened to me in my life, but you have proven to me that I cannot, or will not, ever trust another human being as long as I live. That's how important this was for me. From this moment on, I do not ever want to see your face or hear your voice again. If you see me, I want you to turn and go the other way. I want you to look at every woman you are with from here on out and know that YOU are every girl's 'Brandy.' You are a whore and a disgusting excuse for a human being. No matter what happens in the future, stay the hell away from me."

She then turns and walks back to me, lifts up on her tiptoes and kisses my cheek, saying quietly, "Thank you for being a real man. I wish my dad could have been more like you, teaching me to watch out for guys like him, but then again, my dad truly is the worst human being I know."

I'm in shock as I look at her for a moment, seeing the fighting sparks in her eyes, and I smile at her. I gently squeeze her shoulders and open the front door for her, telling her to try and have a better day and to keep my business card close. I hope she never has to use it.

As I close the door, all eyes are on me, waiting for the explosion they all know is coming their way, in a matter of seconds, by the look on my mad as fuck face. I walk over to Cadence as Archie moves away from him. Cadence looks at me carefully and quietly says, "Sorry about that, boss. I didn't mean to get you involved."

"What exactly are you sorry for, Cadence? Getting caught? Using a young lady for your own pleasure then treating her like garbage afterward? Or is it that when the condom broke, you didn't have the balls to fucking say a goddamn word to her about it? Is it because you being the manwhore that you are, you used my desk to fuck her, and then fuck her world up? What exactly are you sorry for?"

Cadence looks past me and I know that everyone is listening and watching us. Embarrassment takes over his face as he cowers in front of me with my harsh words.

"Not sure, just sorry. Can you please drop it?"

I have no idea what comes over me at Cadence's words, but I shove him back by the shoulders with all my strength, watching him fly back and fall hard, straight on his ass where he belongs. Cadence jumps up and is instantly on the defense, getting in my face. "What the fuck was that for, asshole? I know you have done a lot for me, Des, but don't ever put your fucking hands on me again, old man, 'cause I will knock your old ass out. Got me?"

Wolf instantly appears from behind me, pulling me away from Cadence. "I'm pissed that you can't grow the hell up. She was right, you are a whore that has no respect for himself or anyone else. That is what this is about. I have had enough of your shit, kid, and if you think that you can knock me on my ass, bring it on, Cadence. I might be older than you but I promise you that only one of us will be standing, and that will be me. You're lucky it wasn't Doc, Fern, or one of the kids walking in on you."

Cadence has the decency to put his head down in shame. I push Wolf off me. "I apologize for putting my hands on you, Cadence, that was wrong, but I am so sick of being disappointed in you, especially after how I watched you deal with that situation. It makes me sick to my stomach that you just won't grow the hell up. I'm all for fun, but that young girl is not the usual tramp or bitch that you usually hook up with, is she?" He shakes his head no. "That's what I thought, and now she's lost as hell, walking around with a broken heart and you don't even care. She seemed like a genuinely nice girl, so why go there if your intentions weren't good or honorable. What is wrong with you, Cadence?"

Cadence glares at Des for a minute, then without a word to anyone, turns and walks to the garage, slamming the door behind him.

CHAPTER EIGHT

DES

I turn to head back to my office when I hear Dee Dee's smart-ass remark, "Well, it's nice of you to join us today, Des. Should I assume that you're late because of your long night with the town whore, Katie? And what did I just walk in on between you and Cadence?"

My head jerks back at the animosity in her voice. What the hell is up her ass today? After my run-in with Cadence and the shit with Trinity, I don't need Dee's attitude.

As she makes her way to the counter, Wolf moves to grab the bags and coffee she's carrying. I watch as she gives him a smile and says, "Thanks, honey." Wolf smiles back, caressing her arm and giving her a wink. I watch their interaction, stunned to my core as my blood starts to boil. What the hell is going on with these two? In all the years that they have worked together, I have never seen the two of them so friendly with each other. "Katie wanted me to tell you she had a great time last night. She thought you were a little rough with her, but she really enjoyed it. Oh, and if you find her bra, just give her a call so she can come around to pick it up."

Everyone starts hootin' and howlin' in the office. I should have been prepared for the shitstorm known as Katie. My rejection of her wanting to be something more is causing her to lash out at Dee and that's a problem. Worst of all, I kissed Dee last night. She had no idea Katie had been there, or that I ended things with Katie last night, but it doesn't matter. I fucked up.

Since this is something I will have to work out with Dee in private, I decide I need to get back to business. "Eat your lunch. Once all of you are done, we're having an employee meeting so I can get some shit straight around here. This is not only my business, but also more importantly, my life. Secondly, I need to get your take on something I have been working on for Doc and Fern, so let's get shit moving." Once I say what I need to say, I turn and walk into my office, slamming the door behind me.

I sit down and think on the situation at hand. I know Cadence only ever thinks with his dick, but after the way he treated that girl, leaving her humiliated and worried about her fate, it caused me to lose my mind. Nevertheless, no matter what I know, I had no right to put my hands on the kid. I have no idea what came over me. I have never touched another human being in such a way. Cadence did something I found revolting, but I let my anger get the best of me. Now, to top it all off, I have Dee Dee pissed off and telling everyone in the office about my personal business.

All I can do at this point is wait and talk about everything in the meeting. I put my head in my hands and try to breathe deeply to calm down. All I can do is try to handle one situation at a time.

For what feels like only minutes of trying to find some sort of calm, I hear a knock on the door but before I can say anything, in walks Dee, looking anything but happy to be here. "Can you please approve these orders before I send them out? They're pretty expensive parts so Wolf said to ask for your approval and sign off."

I just stare at Dee until I finally find my voice and ask, "What's going on, Dee Dee? After last night, I thought we were going to consider the possibility of moving forward with one another."

She glares at me with disgust as she says, "What could you possibly be talking about?" Coming around the desk, I walk toward her as she starts moving away from me. "Just approve the orders, Des, so I can be out of your way."

I ignore her, getting in her space as I back her against the file cabinet. I look at her and see that her face is flushed and her breathing is heavy and drawn out. It hits me then that she is aroused, not quite as mad as she wants me to think. I feel the heat coming off her body as I brush up against her, feeling her nipples poking through her blouse onto my chest.

Dee looks up at me once she gets herself under control and smirks at me. "Katie not enough for you last night, Des? Did you fuck her before or after I left?"

I grab her head in both of my hands, making my intentions clear as I stare at her full lips and whisper, "No, Dee. She isn't enough because she isn't you." I slowly lower my head and touch my lips to hers. I wait, not wanting to force myself on her. I slowly move my lips against hers, lightly running my tongue over her full lower lip as she slowly relaxes against me, letting out a long desire-filled moan. As I put more pressure on her lips, she opens them immediately, so I take full advantage as the kiss becomes demanding and I hungrily devour her mouth. I'm making a statement, showing her how much I want her and what I feel for her. I feel her shaking as she shoves me away when someone knocks on the door.

"Boss! When are you going to have this meeting? We all got shit to do, and have you seen Dee Dee? No one knows where she is," Cadence yells through the door. At least he doesn't decide to just walk on in.

"Give me ten minutes. We're in the middle of something, then we'll be out," I yell back at Cadence.

I grab Dee and hold her tight and tell her, "Sugar, don't panic. Don't you dare think too much about this and make this moment into something cheap. This is one of the best days of my life." Then I kiss her lightly on the lips and give her time to get her emotions in check.

"I'm not Katie, Des. I'm not some town tramp for you to use when you need me."

"I can't believe that you would even think that I would look at you in that way. I have nothing but respect for you, Dee baby. I can see that we have a lot to discuss, Sugar, and now just isn't the time. How would you feel about coming over tonight, away from all this drama and just talk? Can we do that?" She takes a moment to think about it, then shakes her head in agreement. Once she is ready, I pull her in for a hug. "Don't make any decision until we talk about the possibilities of our future tonight. I want us to spend some time together and start to get to know each other again, if that works for you."

Dee leans away from me and stares at my face, looking for something. I don't know what it is she finds, but she says, "I'm willing and open to having a serious conversation with you about the possibility of taking anything between us further. The kids will be out tonight, so tonight would be good." I let the breath I'd been holding out and feel so much relief that she's willing to hear me out and keep an open mind.

Now that I have this situation under some sort of control, it's time to get this meeting started.

CHAPTER NINE

DES

As I head down the hallway to the open office in front of the building, I hear a discussion going on about why I'm in such a pissed-off mood. Wolf thinks it has something to do with Katie and my night before. As he says this, I hear Dee Dee make a funny noise in her throat. That's something I need to clarify for her, that Katie is not an issue.

Cadence interjects, telling everyone that I'm mad because he was in my office, screwing a girl on my desk when I walked in. Doc doesn't say anything as he sees me come into the doorway, quietly, just standing there watching and listening to their interaction. "Can I join in? Or am I only allowed to listen to ya'll talk about me behind my back?"

Wolf interjects with a smirk on his face, "Actually, it's to your face, as you're standing right there." I grin at Wolf's smart-ass comment while flipping him the bird. I'm glad that the mood has lightened.

I look around and realize that everyone is here except for Dee's kids. As if she can read my mind, she tells me, "The kids are on their way."

I nod and walk farther into the room and announce to everyone, "Let's wait a couple more minutes for the youth of our crew."

As everyone finishes their lunch, they continue to bicker back and forth with each other. I listen and realize that I love when everyone is here together in a group like this. It makes this horde of people feel like a real family as they share their lives and mess around with each other. I hear the bell over the door ring so I turn around and see Jagger and Daisy entering the building and they both smile my way. I wait for them to have a seat before I begin, "Is Fern going to make it in, buddy?"

Doc looks up, shrugs his shoulders and replies, "As far as I know. We talked about it this morning and she was feeling pretty good. She was going to have the neighbor drive her here and then we would go home together when I finished. I wanted to give her some time to visit with Dee Dee and the girls."

Just as I think we will have to wait a bit more; I look through the windows and see Doc's neighbor Bud's Ford F 150 pulling into the lot. Doc walks out to help Fern out of the big truck, thanking Buddy. He gives her a sweet kiss before they begin walking hand in hand into the building

Once everyone is settled, I clear my throat and look down at the stack of papers in my hands, but before I start, I need to make my apology to Cadence. "Kid, I owe you an apology for earlier. No matter what, no man has the right to put his hands on another man, and I have always tried to instill that in all of you here. I don't know what got into me, but know that I am sorry. I have so much going on right now, but that is no fucking excuse. I promise it will never happen again," then I remember, "Holy shit. Forgot my language, kids. Sorry about that."

I look back at Cadence as he gives me a nod before looking away. "Now on that note, I have to put my foot down with you guys regarding your activities at the workplace during and after business hours. Before you say anything, tell me, Cadence. What would you have done if it had been Daisy, Willow, or even Dee Dee who walked in on you this morning?

"What did I miss?" Daisy asks, as everyone yells, "Nothing!" "Anyway, I know you're all young and having fun but starting today, that shit will not happen again. Not here. Not during work, not after work, or on the weekends. I know ya'll have keys and such, so don't make me take them away from you or put cameras around the shop just to make sure you listen to what I tell you. Find another place to make your shit happen. I am dead serious about this, so next time I find one of you hound dogs in this building doing shit you know not to do, we will have a problem. Understood?" I hear giggles coming from the women as I watch my entire crew nod their heads in understanding.

"Good. Glad to get that handled. Now, for the real

reason we're having this meeting." I look to Doc to take the lead.

Doc looks around at everyone and without hesitation, he drops the bomb. "Unfortunately, Fern's treatments are not working. The last session of chemotherapy hasn't stopped the growth of the cancer. In fact, by what they found on the scans, it actually looks to be growing and spreading."

The mood in the room changes instantly, going deathly quiet. Everyone seems shocked, struggling, as they don't know what to do or say. Fern is softly crying so I gently hand her off to Doc, telling him to sit with her while I finish. Fern raises her eyes to mine and I see that ghost of a smile on her face, making my chest feel heavy with emotion. Everything she can't say is shining in her eyes; gratitude, trust, and love.

"This is not the news that Fern wanted to share with all of us, but we are her family so we need to help out in any way we can. Besides her cancer, their bills are piling up and their home has recently gone into foreclosure." At this news, there are gasps as the girls' hands come to their mouths in shock. They all know how much Doc and Fern love their little home. "Doc and I have had numerous conversations with the bank, and we've tried everything, but they won't budge. Unfortunately, with everything going on, including all the expenses for Fern's treatments, Doc staying in hotels to be close to the hospital, more debts are adding on to those bills, which is another thing causing their house payments to fall short. Doc has been working side jobs when he has the time and selling whatever he has of any value, so when he came to me, I offered to put the business up for collateral, but of course, he and Fern wouldn't hear of it. He only came to me about this because he wanted to ask if they could rent that tiny cabin back in the woods, and that's when I told him that we would come up with a better solution. Besides, that cabin isn't fit for the wildlife in the area, let alone someone like our Fern who is dealing with cancer."

Taking a moment to fill my lungs, I continue, "I have thought on this, making calls to some friends and acquaintances, and this is what we all came up with. Doc and I had a conversation a few weeks ago because before this meeting happened, I needed him to know my plans; to make sure I had his blessing to go forward with it. After we spoke, Doc had a conversation with Fern, giving her the basic information to see if she was on board with it. We also wanted to know if she was up to it, physically and mentally. I've been trying to work on this by myself, but now I need the help of all of you. Hopefully everyone will be willing to step up and make this work for Doc and Fern." I give everyone a look and see they are all paying very close attention.

"After talking to the Asphalt Raiders out west, my MC Brothers, Bear and Stash came up with a perfect way to help Doc out. We're planning a charity ride in Fern's honor and all the proceeds will go to the Murphy's to help them not only keep their home, but to keep them out of bankruptcy." At this announcement, Fern's shoulders start to tremble as she breaks into sobs.

Doc holds her close, but I can see the tears in his eyes too. When I look around, I'm met with tears from the women, while the "men" are trying to look anywhere but at one another to keep anyone from seeing the emotions running across their faces. I try to explain to all of them that this is a huge undertaking, and how they would have support from not only the Asphalt Riders MC, but from town folks and businesses. To finish up, I explain that other MC clubs that I've been affiliated with over the years are on board and already working on getting the word out.

"This will bring in a lot of people from out of state to our little town. Tranquility, Indiana will be bombarded during this charity ride, which in turn will benefit businesses and the entire town. Brick has already started working this out with his MC and brothers from other clubs. They all know Fern's story so they all want to help and be involved."

Grabbing my water, I take a long drink and continue with the rest, "To take this further, I have been in contact with our local Memorial Hospital Cancer Department. We all know Fern really doesn't have any real close family. Knowing that, she is going to need a bone marrow transplant, so during the ride, we are going to be asking that everyone be tested to see if anyone turns up as a match for her. The National Bone Marrow Registry will be present, explaining what is included in testing and donating. What I've gathered from my research is that there are two ways to donate. The first is peripheral blood stem cell collection, and the other is a bone marrow donation. I wanted to make sure we had some background on the process and how this ride could help not only Fern, but others battling this fucking disease."

I walk over to Fern, crouch down, and gently lift her chin. "Sweetheart, you've been fighting so hard, and we don't want you to fight alone any longer. You and Doc are family, and this is what family does for each other."

Fern wipes her tears on her sleeve. "Des, you have torn my heart apart with your actions. It is so full of love for all that you have done. I have never known this kind of unconditional love, besides Gabriel, in my life. I'll admit I'm struggling with the idea of all the work this will put on everyone in this room. We will never be able to pay you back for taking on such a darn... oh, I can't even think of a word to express the size of this undertaking. I don't understand why you have always gone the extra mile for Gabriel and me. Our own blood hasn't been there for us, but you always seem to be the one to carry the load for all of us. You took Doc on as an employee, knowing he had limited skills and that I was sick, wanting and needing the medical insurance. Never have you once given him a hard time with all his coming and going to be with me during my time in and out of the hospital. Thank you seems to be such inappropriately simple words and do not express our eternal gratitude. Both of us are forever in your debt, Desmond."

I go to stand up when Doc grabs my shoulders. "Brother, I have no fucking words."

"None needed, brother. I already know." I then walk to the center of the room and ask my crew, "Are you all in or what?" They all raise their hands, ready to do whatever they can to help. These people are my family by my own choice.

CHAPTER TEN

DES

3 Months Later

My life has taken a couple of turns, personally and professionally. My relationship with Dee is going great. We spend as much time together as we can. We finally told her kids, who were as happy as pigs in shit. They both like me and want to see their mother happy. Everyone at the shop seems to know what is going on with us, but they have kept their comments to themselves.

The announcement of the Charity Ride for Fern has really taken off. I was pleasantly surprised at how everyone started working together to get this ride organized. Everyone has contributed. No matter how small or large, all have been a blessing. The raffle has things from haircut gift certificates to the local Harley dealership offering a full set of leathers, along with a gift certificate for new tires and a tune-up. The biggest donation came from the local car dealership, raffling off a base model car. This was huge. If you can name it, it was donated.

Now that the Registry for Bone Marrow is on board, they are advertising the ride, also asking people to stop at certain stops along the ride to register and be tested. Even if a match isn't found for Fern, their donation might save someone else's life. The people I've been dealing with at the Registry are truly wonderful folks.

With this entire undertaking of the charity ride going on, I'm always watching Fern. She's not quite getting worse, but she's not getting any better, either. Her health hasn't been strong for a while, but she's really trying to be strong, trying to show everyone if they think she's worth fighting for, then she's gonna keep fighting. Between her treatments not working and her body breaking down on her, this event couldn't be happening at a better time.

"Have you heard anything from Trinity, boss?" The question catches me off guard, so I have to take a minute to think of who Trinity is, and then it hits me. She was the hookup I walked in on about three months ago.

"No, as a matter of fact I haven't, kid. I told her to get in touch with me if she needed anything, but I haven't seen or heard from her, so I assumed everything was okay. I also never thought to check with everything going on around here. What's the reason for you to ask me now?" The kid drops his head and looks defeated, so I ask again when he doesn't answer, "What the hell's going on now, Cadence? I can't help you if you don't talk to me."

Cadence looks right into my eyes and angrily tells me, "I'm going to be a daddy I've been told but I can't find the baby's momma. How's that for what's going on, Des?"

Well, I can't say that I'm surprised. I sit back and let him glare at me. I can't believe I forgot about the incident and never thought to check on the outcome, but that was Cadence's responsibility, not mine, so he can look at me like that as long as he wants. He fucked up, not me.

Cadence has been acting distracted lately, and as far as I know, he hasn't been bringing his usual stash of bar bitches back to his place or going out much. He comes to work, helps with the charity ride, or goes to his apartment upstairs. I also noticed that he's been doing a lot of work on his apartment upstairs recently, bringing in stuff to fix it up.

He's one of the most immature men I know, who gets what he wants when he wants it, but no one knows that the kid has a real soft side. People don't know that he spends his free time coaching kids' baseball and soccer games. He always makes a stop at the pediatric floor of the hospital after each of his visits with Fern when she's there. He hangs out and spends time with the sickest children, bringing board games for them all to play. If there is a chance that he's going to be a daddy, I really hope that he wants to be involved, even if he and the mother aren't together. He craves acceptance and love, and it's only when you truly watch him that you see it.

"So how do you know she's pregnant?"

"A friend of hers saw me in the bathroom at the bar getting a blow job from one of their friends about four days ago. I've been asking around about her, but her friends haven't been back to the bar in months, and no one would tell me anything, saying they didn't know shit. I don't even know where she lives or works. I ran out of the bathroom to chase her friend down, I guess so I could try and explain myself, and that I haven't heard a word from Trinity in months. I asked her if she could tell me if she was okay. That's when her friend turned around and slapped the shit out of me, telling me Trinity wasn't okay after what I did to her and that no self-respecting mother-to-be would show her face in a bar. Des, I was floored, but I know this is my responsibility if the baby is mine, so I asked her if it was and she punched me in the chest, calling me a stupid, pathetic asshole. I mean, what the fuck? It was just an honest question I told her, then she punched me *again*. She screamed out in front of the entire bar that Trinity isn't a whore—that I was only the second man she had ever been with. After being beaten by a woman and made to feel like shit, I demanded Trinity's address. She spit on me then turned and walked away. So, I have a chick who I fucked and knocked up, who I can't even begin to find because either no one knows or no one will tell me. I reached out to that shrink. I have been seeing Dr. Joe for a couple of weeks now. She's actually helping me get some perspective in my life, but now I feel like I'm losing control again."

"Cadence, I'm sorry about this whole situation. You gotta know that you can always come to me and know that if there is anything I can do to help, I'm here for you."

Cadence just shakes his head. With my hands resting on his shoulders, I feel him start to shake, realizing the kid is actually crying. Grabbing him into a tight hug, he hugs me back even tighter, just letting it all go.

"Fuck, Des. I am such a fuckup. All I ever think about is myself. What am I gonna do? I don't want my kid growing up without a dad. I know how much that sucks. I have to find her and my baby, Des. Please, can you help me?

"Let me see what I can do. I'll call a couple of my buddies and see if we can find her, but, Cadence? If she doesn't want to be found, we won't find her, so prepare yourself for that, okay? Also, I think you need to see Dr. Joe more frequently. I think she'll be able to help you deal with this shit you've got going on in your head. I don't know your story kid, but I do know that until you deal with the past, you have no future." He shakes his head and wipes his face. He turns to leave but I clear my throat. "Kid, you aren't alone. You have family here who would do anything for you."

"Yeah, I know," he says. I pat his shoulder as he leaves the room.

After he's gone, I reach for the phone because there

is one person who can always help Cadence put things into perspective. "Fern? It's me. How you feeling, honey? That's good, I'm glad to hear it. Listen, I need to bring you up to speed with Cadence. He's got himself in quite a mess, and I just want to warn you that he's gonna need you."

CHAPTER ELEVEN

CADENCE

As night falls, I sit in my apartment alone. I look around at all the work I've done to make my apartment feel more like a home than just a place to lay my head. I'm finally starting to understand why people want to take pride in their homes, and by the looks of this place now, I can see my hard work is really paying off. The kitchen is done with new cabinets, granite countertops, and stainless-steel appliances. I've even gone as far as to pull up the old laminate flooring, replacing it with hardwood floors all throughout the apartment. The floors turned out perfect and they shine throughout the place. This was a job in itself because my apartment is huge, covering the entire top of Connelly's Wheels & Hogs. Even though I don't remember the exact footage, it's mammoth. Besides the kitchen, I have an eating nook with huge windows, a dining room, and a family room off the kitchen with an island between the two rooms. I also have three bedrooms with two baths and an office.

For someone like me it's a lot, but since Des refuses to ever take rent money, I figured this was a good way to pay him back. When I eventually move, Des will be able to rent this place for a pretty steep price. I've also remodeled both bathrooms with ceramic tile and new updated fixtures. All colors throughout the apartment are muted, except my bedroom. As I walk down the hallway to my room, I rub my hands through my hair, feeling extremely lonely.

My bedroom is a vibrant blue with gray accents. The room is completed with a black dresser and matching nightstands to go with my huge, four-poster bed right in the middle. If anyone saw my work up here, they wouldn't think the smart-ass manwhore did the work and picked out the colors. This side of myself I like to keep from others.

I lie down on the bed and try to relax, but I can't stop my mind from thinking of my past and of Trinity being pregnant. Even though the most important thing to think about is Trinity and the baby, Duke always takes over, filling my mind with all the horrid things that happen to people—all the horrid things that happened to me. God, I hate that motherfucker. I wish I could find him, then slowly kill him for all the pain he brought to my family and me.

My mind starts to wander back to the time I was held by Duke against my will. I had no idea what was going on when I woke up in that cabin alone, cuffed to a bed frame. I freaked out trying to break free, but I couldn't. For hours, I tried to wiggle and pull, everything I could do to get free, even tearing the skin from my wrists and ankles until they were raw and bleeding. When the door opened and Duke walked in, my heart actually felt like it stopped. The look in my stepfather's eyes was one of complete and utter madness. He casually walked to the side of the bed asking me, "How are you doing, son?" I felt the vomit in my mouth at the word *son*.

I looked Duke in the eyes and said, "I ain't your son, asshole." Duke proceeded to beat on me for hours, reminding me that he could call me whatever he wanted to, but more importantly, do whatever he wanted to do to me. He told me from that moment on, I was his own little bitch. He left me alone, leaving for a bit. I had to humiliate myself because I had needed to release my bladder for hours. When I finally couldn't hold it any longer, I felt the warmth run under me, onto the bed and down my legs, feeling less than a man because I couldn't control my bladder.

When Duke returned, he removed the cuffs, instructing me to clean myself up and to change the bed. I found a bunch of sheets on a shelf in the bathroom, so I changed the sheets first and then washed up. My body was bruising from the beating I'd just taken. Looking in the mirror, I didn't even recognize myself. Both of my eyes were swollen shut, my face and body covered in bruises and scratches.

When I came out of the bathroom, I saw that my

nightmare was truly just beginning. Duke was naked on the bed, his hand running up and down his cock. His cold ruthless eyes stared into mine as he grinned. "Get your fine ass over here, boy. I have been waiting to do this to you forever, saving the best for last," he laughed. My heart did stop as I ran for the door, but Duke beat me to it, pulling me as I fought and screamed while he dragged me back to the bed. The next few hours of my life were a living hell. I screamed, fought, scratched, drew blood with my teeth, but I couldn't get away from him. When Duke was finally finished with me, I thought I was going to lie there and bleed to death, feeling like my life was flowing out of every part of my body, but to my utter horror, he patched me up.

Duke repeatedly told me if he allowed me to live, I was never to tell anyone about this or he would kill my mother and Griffin would experience a much worse fate. This went on for days or weeks, I had no idea how much time, as I begged Duke to end my life. I hit an all-time low when Duke brought some *friends* to participate. He explained that they were there to join in on the party with me. The things they made me do ruin me not only physically, but mentally. After the men took what they wanted from me, I became nothing; a worthless, disgusting no one. I couldn't wrap my shattered mind around the idea that people could do these things to me, knowing that I wasn't willing in any way, turned my stomach. Those sick, perverted men were not human beings at all; they were monsters, just like Duke.

I finally passed out, waking up in a field having no idea where I was. I couldn't move between the beatings and repeated abuse that those men had done to my body. I figured that death would find me in that field. After what I had just gone through, I begged, accepted, and waited for my death to come, but that wasn't to be. When Des found me, I was so pissed off at him because I wanted to die, not be saved. Des took that away from me, but as time passed, I realized how fortunate this turn of events was for me. Between Des, Doc, and Fern, I started to heal physically.

Emotionally was another story. I was crippled until Fern took me under her wing. From holding me night after night because of my nightmares, to just being there for me to lean on, she pushed me to seek professional help when she knew she and Doc could not help me any longer. My pain was too deep, and I was just too damaged emotionally for them to fix. I did seek out help back then and have continued to do so on numerous occasions since, especially when the nightmares come or life is just too hard to handle. Sometimes it just gives me some sort of direction in my life when I need it the most.

Fern became the mother that I needed. After the incident with Duke, I wouldn't... no, I couldn't speak to my own mother. I blamed her for everything because she brought Duke into our lives. Fern fought to make me better. She protected and guided me, and I love her deeply. When she got sick, I felt like my heart was being pulled from my body. I have spent many of my nights in the hospital, or in the Murphy's house with Doc, doing whatever I could do to help with Fern. There is nothing I wouldn't do for her. Between changing her sheets when needed, to helping with the house chores, I have also cooked and fed Fern, even driving her to and from her treatments. She is the embodiment of a pure soul. I always feel my best when I'm in the company of Fern and Doc.

I sit up in my bed, holding my head as it starts to pound. My body begins to tense up tight as the thoughts of my past begin to take a firm hold over me, causing me to feel the familiar aches in my muscles while my eyes start to twitch. I push off the bed and walk to my bathroom to take the medication Doc gave me for my type of headache. I take one with some water then walk to the kitchen to get some food in my stomach. The medicine is so strong; I have to eat to keep from getting sick. I grab some of Fern's pasta that she brought to me and throw it in the microwave.

After the microwave dings off, I pull out the food and at the same time, I hear a sound coming from outside. It's pitch-black out, so I grab a flashlight and head out down the stairs. Once I get to the bottom of the steps, I can hear the noise coming from behind the dumpster. Whatever it is, it's making a lot of noise, so I walk cautiously toward the sound. I move the flashlight back and forth when something moves on my right, so I aim the beam in that direction, only to see four eyes staring back at me. I crouch down and snap my fingers softly, watching those four eyes attached to two straggly looking kittens slowly coming toward me. They watch me closely and I don't move. After a few moments, they finally make it to me and begin smelling the hand I'm holding out to them. I sit down slowly and wait for them to do what they need to do. Finally the little black one bumps up against me, looking up at me expectantly, while the other kitten is on my other side, rubbing up against my leg. Almost at the same time, they both leap into my lap and I can't help the huge smile that takes over my mouth. It looks like I've made some new friends.

CHAPTER TWELVE

CADENCE

After the first couple of days of not knowing what to do with my new, unnamed friends, I asked Wolf to stop by my apartment. He didn't ask questions, but I could see he was curious with my request.

When Wolf arrives, I offer him a beer and lead him to the small bedroom, where I show him the two kittens. When I open the door, they both escape down the hall and into the family room like tiny missiles, all short legs and hair. I shout for Wolf to grab one as we both race after them. We enter the family room just in time to see the kittens climbing up the leather couch with their dagger claws assisting in their upward approach. Wolf very gently grabs the smallest kitten and cuddles it close to his chest. It snuggles up right under his chin, immediately starting to purr while the larger kitten continues to climb up onto the couch. Wolf grabs that one too and sits down, putting both of them in his lap.

"Damn, Cadence. What have you got here?" Wolf lets out a soft laugh. "What are these little cuties' names?"

I shake my head. "No idea, dude. I'm lost here. If you want them, you can take them because I don't have a clue what I'm doing. I found them a couple of nights ago and I've been on the internet trying to figure out what I'm supposed to do to take care of them."

Shaking his head back and forth, Wolf says, "No way, bro. My house is overrun with too many orphaned animals as it is. Spirit keeps bringing home stray animals all the time." Spirit is the dog Wolf saved from an abusive owner a couple of years ago, and now Spirit's home is with Wolf. "Let's take a look at these kittens first, okay?" The larger one is mainly gray with a few white strips on its back and belly. Wolf looks up at me as he lifts it up, "This one is a male, so name him Kibble." The smaller one has white paws that look like socks on its feet, while the rest of it is black, "This one is a male too, and he should be called Boots, don't you think?"

I just shake my head, completely lost. "Dude, I have no idea how to take care of them. They are tearing my place apart and I worked my ass off fixing it up. I went down to the store and grabbed some of those cans of soft cat food and that's it. The only reason I got that right is because it said *cat food*. I've figured out what to feed them, and now they seem to piss and shit all the time in that box I bought. They won't go outside and do it, so this place is starting to reek of piss and shit."

Wolf's shoulders shake as he lets out a loud laugh. "Okay kid, take it easy. Shit, I thought you were the expert on pussy." I flip him the bird as he continues to laugh. "First off, let's put them back in the room so we can kitty proof your house. Then we will go out and pick up the things they will need, okay?" Wolf walks with both kittens in his arms to the room, gently putting them down before closing the door.

Both of us go through the apartment, making sure nothing is available for the kittens to get into. Wolf puts the throws that are on the back of the couch over the furniture's cushions, tucking them in so they partly hang down to the floor.

"This will let them climb up to be with you, but not ruin the furniture. Understand?" I just nod. After going through the whole apartment, Wolf approves of what we've done to make it kitty proof.

"You got time to run to the pet store, or do you have some lady waiting on you?"

"I got no one waiting on me, so yeah, let's go to the store, if ya don't mind." Then off we go to get what I need for my little house destroyers.

After approximately forty-five minutes in the pet store, we roll a shopping cart filled with food, litter, toys, and a scratching post out to the truck. I can't believe how much this shit cost. We load up the truck then head back to my place. Between the two of us, we set up the scratching post tower, put the bowls on the placemat in the kitchen, and set up the other litter box in a corner by the sliding doors to the patio. Wolf then grabs each kitten to show them the bowls, the scratching post, and then the litter boxes. After around ten minutes of investigating, both kittens climb up onto the couch and fall asleep next to each other on the corner of a cushion.

"So that's it? I spend a shitload of money to make this place suitable for them and they just pass out?"

"Bro, with any animal, they are just like babies. They depend on you for everything because they can't do these things for themselves. You ever see a dog go shopping for his food? You ever see them jump up on the toilet because it's the right thing to do? No, you don't. You're like their mother and they will continue to bond with you, and each other, every day. Just make sure to clean their litter boxes at least twice a day, kid. Also, keep dry food out for them and give them like a quarter can each of the soft canned food. The more you handle them the friendlier they will be. I'll come back and help you trim their nails. If you keep them trimmed there is less chance of being clawed all the time, and less damage to your floors and furniture. Now, if you don't plan on keeping them, take them to the shelter so someone will adopt them, but know this, too. The longer you keep them, the more they will become attached to one another, and if you do decide to take them to a shelter, they probably won't get adopted together. Just a thought before you make any decisions."

"Nothing has ever depended on me before, Wolf. Not anything or anyone. Some part of me kind of likes the idea of being responsible for something other than myself, though. Do you think I can do this? Ya know, be responsible for them? Take care of them by myself?"

Wolf looks at me for a long time. His stare makes me squirm, not really liking what he's possibly seeing in me right now. He walks toward me, putting both hands on my shoulders. "Cadence, I think if you put your mind to anything brother, you can do it. Do you want to keep the kids?" My head jerks up at Wolf's play on words. Does he know about Trinity, or is this just my guilt coming through? I look over to the kittens cuddling together on the couch and I know that I want to keep them. I never had any pets growing up because I wasn't allowed. They are both so cute and playful, but more importantly, they need me. I feel this is a moment in my life that I need to take a chance.

Going to the kittens, I reach down and slowly pet them as I say to Wolf, "Yes. I want to keep them and thank you for all of your help tonight. I'll probably be coming to you with tons of questions for a while, so I hope you won't mind."

Wolf grins. "Not at all, kid. That's what I'm here for, buddy. Just call, and I'll be available for you anytime, bro."

We both sit down and reach for our beers as I turn on the TV. For once in my life I feel like I have a true home; my home. Wolf stays around for take-out Chinese food, trying to give me some direction and advice on how to feed the kittens while showing me how to maintain the litter boxes. We arrange the kitty houses in the small bedroom, so they have somewhere to sleep when I have to put them in there when I need to be at work. We also put little pet cushions around the apartment so they can be comfortable anywhere they are.

After Wolf leaves, I clean up the night's mess then get ready for bed. Once I set my alarm for work and settle in, I hear a very soft whining, then another. I look down to see Kibble and Boots sitting on the floor by my bed, looking up at me with big eyes. Kibbles' eyes are green, while Boots's are blue. I reach down to pick them both up and immediately they each pick a side, cuddling up next to me. Before my head touches the pillow, both kittens are sound asleep.

For once in my life, I feel contentment in my heart, something foreign and new to me. If only I could find Trinity and straighten that part of my life out, especially now that I know she's pregnant with my child. Even with thoughts of Trinity and the baby, I am finally able to drift off to sleep with no nightmares, and the warmth of my tiny little kittens each at my side.

CHAPTER THIRTEEN

DES

As I enter the bay, I notice that Cadence seems to be in a great mood. He probably got laid last night. I continue toward the kid, watching him work on the engine of a car and I hear music in the background. I listen to the song and find myself actually liking it, "Hey, kid. Who's that you're listening to?"

Cadence lifts his head to hear the song. "Some band out of Las Vegas called Otherwise. Pretty good, huh? They played in some bar in South Bend last summer. A bunch of us went to see them and I got hooked on their music."

I listen to the words for a minute, a song with the lyrics. "*I don't apologize for taking back the life that I once had,*" and I have to agree with Cadence. "They're not bad at all. If they come around again, let me know. I might be interested in seeing them."

Cadence raises his eyebrows at this. "You gonna

jump in the mosh pit too, Des?" As I shake my head, he just laughs.

"Cadence, you got a minute? We need to touch base on where we are with the charity ride and the Registry. We only have until the end of summer to make sure all our arrangements are set. here's not a lot of time left and with all the people involved, I don't want anything to slip past any of us."

~Cadence~

Des and I both head back to Des's office, which is filled with everyone from the shop, including our town sheriff, Joe Hound, and some of the town council, along with business owners from town. I'm shocked to see all these folks here. I had no idea that all these people were helping with Fern's ride. I find an empty chair and take a seat.

Dee stands at the front of the room and begins, "This is a huge undertaking, and we thank each and every one of you who have volunteered your time, business, or some financial assistance to both Fern and Doc. We can't thank you enough. I know everyone has things to do so we'll get down to business."

As Dee starts going through list after list of what has been done, what is outstanding, and who is doing what, my head starts to pound and spin. How does she keep it all together? Everyone is involved, asking questions, and giving suggestions. After around two hours of this, Dee has given out all the work orders to finish up the preparations for the charity ride, and more importantly, the Registry to try and find a match for Fern.

Des rises and takes on a serious demeanor and asks everyone for just a moment more of their time. "We have received a couple of warnings and threats in regards to this charity event." My head jerks up as I hear others gasp. "Joe is looking into it but with these threats, we have decided to bring in some outside security to maintain that all are safe during this weekend event." Joe doesn't look too happy about this news, but Des explains that he has called some of his old biker friends to come out early and assist them. Des goes a bit further by explaining that his friends are not one-percent bikers, but cops who formed a motorcycle club. They have the experience as they run a security business out west. All the guys agree that it is the right move to make, having the extra help on hand as the threats seem to be concentrated toward the money the ride will raise for the Murphy's. Des doesn't want to go through all this and have some assholes rip us off, so after speaking with his friends and Sheriff Joe, they all agreed that Joe was in charge of security but would have some assistance of ten to fifteen of the best security/cops from out west. Des warns everyone to be extra careful and keep their eyes open for any strangers, or if we should see anything out of the ordinary. The funds being raised from ticket sales and donations are in an account in the town bank and from what Dee stated earlier, the account is growing by the day. With the local news now on this story, people are donating directly to the bank. Des closes out the meeting by thanking everyone for their time, informing them that they will be meeting every week going forward until the weekend of the ride.

I wait until everyone has left the office to ask Des a question that has been bothering me for a few days now. "Hey, Des? Have you heard anything from your guy about Trinity?"

Des motions for me to sit down as he leans his elbows on his desk. "I wanted to talk to you about that, kid. I found her, but I feel as if I should point this out to you. If she wanted to see or talk to you, I think she would have reached out to you by now, but she hasn't. I don't think after the way you treated her that she wants anything to do with you. Maybe she feels that you showed her you're not exactly 'Daddy' material and she's decided to do this alone. You didn't give her a reason to think that you would want to be any part of it."

I can feel my temper start to rise. "When the hell did you find her? Shit, why am I just finding this out? Fuck, Des! She's pregnant with my kid for Christ's sake."

Des looks at me with pity, but also a lot of anger. "Let's be very honest here, kid. You weren't thinking about that when you fucked her on this very desk, with no concern as to what could happen. I watched you stare at that ripped condom and not even give her the courtesy of telling her what had just happened. Instead, you treated her like a piece of ass to help you get through your afternoon. Not once in these three months have you put any real, honest-to-God effort into finding her to check on her; see if she needed you. This wasn't all on her, Cadence. You both made a choice and you, kid, seriously fucked up. You kept up with your fuck 'em and leave 'em bullshit. How many women have you fucked since that day, huh? Can't answer? That's my point exactly. It wasn't until her friend knocked you around did you even give a second thought of the mother of your child, so cut the bullshit with me, kid, 'cause I ain't buying it."

"I know that I'm a fuckup, Des, but believe it or not I'm not trying to run from my responsibility—not anymore. I need to find her and make her see how sorry I am." My entire body is shaking, and I feel like I'm about to have a massive anxiety attack.

Des reaches forward to grab me by the shoulders, trying to help ground me. Speaking softly, he says, "Listen, my guy found out that she is living with some old fucker in the mobile home park on the other side of town. She hasn't been seen in a while, so no one knows what is going on. Some of my guys are taking turns staking out the trailer park, trying to get a fix on the situation. Right now, that is all I know. I don't know who the fucker is that she's living with, and I have no other knowledge or information to give you. Sorry, kid, but that's what it is right now."

I nod my head, realizing this isn't Des's fault. We stand and make our way to the door. "Please keep me in the loop, Boss, okay?"

"Sure, kid. You'll be the first to know when I find anything out."

I go back to the shop to finish the car I was working on before the meeting started. As I work, my mind wanders to Trinity. God, she was something. She had an innocence around her that drew me to her. She was the one girl I could just enjoy hanging out and relaxing with. We both loved to dance and karaoke. Sometimes just grabbing a beer after work with her, bitching to each other about our days was a luxury for me. Even though I spent time with Trinity, I was still sleeping with every slut and bar bitch in town, but she was different, and I never thought of using her that way.

Having sex with her for the first time was the most amazing experience. She was beautiful, sexy, and so trusting of me, but the when I screwed her on Des's desk and saw the condom was ripped because of *my* fucking piercings, I panicked and checked out. All I knew was that I had to get out of there, but in doing that, I left Des there to deal with her and to clean up another one of my messes... again. Even now, after all my stupid and immature decisions, Des is helping me to try and fix this shit. No, not fix it, but trying to see past that and look at the man I am trying to be. I need to be there for Trinity and my baby.

All I know is that I want the chance to apologize to her and be a part of my kid's life. I hope that Des and his friends can help me. I need all the help I can get right now.

CHAPTER FOURTEEN

DES

Dropping my phone on the kitchen table, I look up to see Dee Dee staring at me, looking concerned.

"What's up, Des? You look worried."

I grab her hands gently, rubbing my fingers over the top of her hands. "Damn, honey. We got trouble. Not sure how much, but more importantly, I'm not sure how Cadence is gonna handle this."

"Is this about that young girl, Trinity? Is she in some kind of trouble?"

"That was one of my guys who's been keeping an eye on that trailer park I told you they found Trinity in. He said that she finally stepped out of the trailer after the old guy left this morning." I run my fingers through my hair. "Fuck, Dee! He said her face was black and blue, and any body part showing was bruised all to hell. Her eyes were swollen shut, lip split. He also said she looks to be skin and bones. She's fucking pregnant, into her second trimester by now, and she looks like that? What do I do, Dee Dee?

The kid is going to lose his shit, and who the fuck is that old motherfucker she's living with? He's obviously the one beating the shit out of her, so what else is he doing to her?"

Dee takes a minute to think, then squeezes my hand and explains, "We need to do whatever we can to help her. God, Des. We can't just leave her there. Call Cadence now and tell him to get over here. We need to make a plan to get her out of that hell she's living in."

I pick up my phone, doing exactly what Dee tells me to. We wait for Cadence to arrive so we can tell him what is going on, and what we plan to do about it.

~Cadence~

I arrive forty minutes after I got a call from Des, asking me to come over because he has some news. As I enter, I give Dee a quick kiss on the cheek and she gently reaches for my face. I see something in her eyes that makes the hairs on the back of my neck stand up. "What's going on, guys? Something wrong?"

I watch Des go to the fridge and grab three beers then head to the family room. "Take a seat, kid," he says as he pushes a beer toward me. "I think you're going to need this."

I sit and listen to all that Des has to tell me, feeling my anger build and build. Fuck! What the hell has

Trinity gotten herself into? She's carrying my kid inside of her and she's letting herself be beaten? Why the fuck hasn't she called me for help to get her out of whatever mess she's in? Maybe it's because this kid isn't mine after all. Why I even think up such a ridiculous idea, I have no idea. I just know that I'm scared, pissed, and thinking like an asshole.

I realize that Des has stopped talking, so I look up and see both of them staring at me, waiting for me to say something. "WHAT? I don't even know what the fuck you both want me to say."

Dee glares at me. "Do you even care that she's being abused, Cadence?"

I look at Dee, feeling the anger in me coming to the surface. "What fucking kind of question is that Dee Dee? Do you think that low of me? Do you?"

Dee Dee's body jerks like I just slapped her as Des jumps to his feet, grabbing me by my shirt. "Don't you ever talk to her like that again, you little shit. Do ya hear me?"

"Let him go, honey. He didn't mean anything by it, did you, Cadence?"

"Shit. I didn't mean any of it. I'm sorry for the shit I spewed to you, Dee. That was so fucking uncalled for and I'm so sorry."

Des lets me go and puts his arm around Dee to pull her close to his side, glaring at me. "Well, this one is on you. What're we going to do to help this girl, kid? It's your call."

I look right into Des's eyes. "We need to get her out of there Des, no matter what. That's where we start."

Des reaches for his phone and speaks with a guy named Matty, the guy staking out the trailer. He asks him a few questions and hangs up. "Okay. The old fucker isn't there. Matty had one of the other guys follow him to a bar in town, so it's now or never. We need to go get her out of there and we don't have a lot of time. Before we do this, we need to understand that we could be bringing some major shit down on us, without any knowledge of this old fucker and the situation. I have a bad feeling about him and it's not just because he's beating her. If you're ready to handle what could come knocking on our door, then I'll let Matty know to call in some guys so we can get this done tonight." We all three agree and Des makes the call.

Des pulls his king cab truck up behind Matty's Mustang. We all get out of our vehicles, meeting around the back of the truck. Matty is a guy who apparently likes to work out a lot. Another car pulls up, as three guys get out and walk toward us. Des gives them a nod and introduces them to us, "This is Mike, Drew, and Toby. Guys, this is Dee and Cadence."

We all nod at one another when Matty starts to talk, "She's alone and George is at the bar, watching the old asshole so he doesn't surprise us."

We all leave the vehicles on the street, walking toward the trailer Trinity is staying in.

~Dee Dee~

I walk up the stairs with Cadence as he knocks on the badly rotting door. We wait a few minutes before he knocks again until we hear a noise from inside and a soft, "*Just a minute.*" We listen as she unlocks the door and opens it just a crack. She looks up, sees Cadence, and slams the door closed, locking it shut.

He bangs on the door. "Trinity! Open this fucking door right now. We don't have much time."

The guys grab Cadence, pulling him off the small porch as Toby jumps up and kicks the door wide open, causing Trinity to scream. I enter the trailer and the smell hits me immediately. I'm not sure what it is that's making my stomach heave, but I go toward the terrified young girl. Holding my hand out, I reach for Trinity. "Hi, honey. I don't know if you know me, but I'm Dee Dee. I work at the garage that Cadence works at. We're here to help you, Trinity, so please don't be afraid of us."

As she lifts her head, I'm shocked at the brutal slit right down the middle of her full lips. Her arms are folded around her stomach with dark bruises on every inch of skin. You can actually see the deep handprints bruised into her upper arms, but what catches my eyes is the way she has her arms folded over her belly. She is protecting her little one the only way she can.

I walk to her carefully and softly repeat, "We are here to help you, Trinity. Please, I'm begging you. Let us help you."

I wait patiently as Trinity stares at me, and then she finally lets out a ragged breath and falls forward, right into my arms while sobbing uncontrollably. I hold her tight and let her have the release she desperately needs. Trinity's whole body shakes violently as she continues to cry and the guys wait patiently while she sobs. Looking at each of the men, I can see this is tearing at their hearts. No young girl should have to go through this.

She continues to cry, and we all take a look around the trailer. We are all shocked at the filth that covers the floor, countertops, and even the furniture. Between rotting food, blood splatters that I would assume came from Trinity, and the smell of urine, none of us can wait to get out of this hellhole.

When she finally gets her tears under control, I push her hair back and use my own T-shirt to wipe the tears and snot off her face before Des, Cadence, and Matty come forward.

Des looks around me and into Trinity's eyes. "Sweetheart, you had my number. You should have called me and I would have helped you. I told you if you needed anything, and I meant that." Matty bumps both men and looks at his watch. Des quietly tells Trinity to let me help her get her stuff together because we are taking her out of here. She starts to shake as tears begin to fall down her cheeks again, telling us that he will find her and punish her again. I'm holding her tight when the first words out of Cadence's mouth are, "Who the fuck is he, Trinity?"

She raises her tear-filled eyes to him and says, "My father."

~Des~

I'm shocked. What father does this to one of their own? I remember my parents, who would have done anything for their children, and here's Trinity's dad, beating on his precious daughter—who's pregnant—and couldn't care less about her. Fuck, what a mess. We still don't know what we're going to do with her once we get her out of here, "Okay, I'm ready." I look around, telling everyone to meet at my house in approximately thirty minutes. They all agree and move to leave. Trinity takes a last look around then heads out following Dee to my truck.

As she goes to get in, Cadence tries to give her a hand, but she quickly pulls out of his reach. I see this, knowing this is going to be a rough fucking night, and here it starts because the kid doesn't take the rejection well. "What the fuck, Trinity? All I wanted to do was give you a hand up."

"Don't you think you've given me enough already? I don't need or want anything else from you, Cadence Powers. I don't need help from a boy who pretends to be a man. Stay the hell away from me."

After arriving home, I put a call in to Doc to come take a look at Trinity. Once he arrives, Dee, Cadence, and I sit quietly as Doc examines Trinity across the room. A very pale Fern is holding her hand as Doc talks to her, asking her questions. She looks exhausted but continues to listen to both of them. Doc is moving her arms to the front, then back, lifting while poking her sides. On her left side, when Doc pokes her there, she grimaces, so Doc asks more questions, waiting for her reply. He listens to her heart then puts the stethoscope to her belly.

We all wait until Doc is done. Fern stands up, asking me if she could help Trinity take a shower. I tell her to use the master bath as Fern leads her down the hall. Doc walks over to us, shaking his head angrily. "She is in pretty bad shape. Besides the obvious bruising, I'd like to get her eyes checked as they're both swollen shut for the most part and her pupils don't look right to me. She might have a broken rib or two on the left side. She's extremely malnourished, but what worries me the most is that she hasn't been to an obstetrician yet. I am very concerned for her baby. I strongly suggest that we get her some professional help, guys, and soon. The only positive I see is that the baby is still small and protected in her uterus. Hopefully that has helped the baby with the beatings that poor girl has been receiving."

"So, what's the plan?" I look at each of them. "I have a bad feeling that this is going to bring trouble from her old man. She can't stay at Dee's, or with you and Fern, as you both live in town. I don't think it's appropriate that she stay at my house here, and I'm pretty sure she's not going to want to stay with Cadence, so our choices are limited. I called someone to see if they could take in another abused soul." As I finish, the sliding door opens and in walks Wolf.

Cadence shoots to his feet. "No fucking way is she staying with him! Absolutely no fucking way—" We listen as he continues on with his ridiculous temper tantrum, "Des, you know how he is with women. There is no way in hell that I'll allow her to go anywhere with him."

"We came out here to get some of her clothes before her shower," says Fern, but Trinity is already walking straight toward Cadence, never taking her swollen eyes from him.

"Who the fuck do you think you are? You have absolutely no say in what I do, where I go, or who I stay with. You will never have any say in what happens to my baby and me!" As her body shakes with so much rage, she turns and walks to Fern, then Fern leads her out of the room. Cadence looks like she just kicked him in his balls. I push him down into the chair then look at Wolf and explain the situation.

Only Wolf, Cadence, and I live outside of our little

town so I figure it would be best to keep Trinity under wraps for a while so no one can locate her. As we continue on with our conversation, the doorbell rings and the other guys enter. As they all grab somewhere to sit, Dee goes to the fridge to grab beers and Cokes for everyone, then goes back to the kitchen and begins pulling out pans and the toaster. I look up at her with a question in my eyes that she answers with, "Honey, she probably hasn't had a good meal in a while. I'm going to make her some scrambled eggs with toast." I nod and move back to the conversation at hand.

~Fern~

In the master bedroom, I help a trembling Trinity dress and make a mental note of all her injuries. Her father should be shot for what he has done to his daughter.

Once she is dressed, I sit her on Des's bed, grabbing a brush—probably Dee's—and start to brush through all the tangles in her hair. Neither of us speaks but it's comforting all the same. Once all the knots are brushed out, I blow-dry it. Since she came here with bare feet, I go to the chest and pull out a pair of men's socks. Bending down, I place the socks on her feet.

"No one has ever taken care of me. Thank you so much."

"I'm here for you if you need anything, okay?" The

young woman just nods, and I continue, "I know right now you're pretty angry and upset at Cadence but remember it's him who had Des start the search for you because he was worried."

Trinity looks up. "It's been three months. Has he been looking for me all this time?

I have nothing to say to that because the answer is no. He only just started looking for her when he found out about the baby, as far as I know.

"No, I didn't think so. Please don't try to make him out to be some hero that he's not."

"He didn't handle this situation well at all, but I know that he is concerned for both you and the baby," I reply. Trinity shakes her head as her belly starts to growl. I laugh as I say, "Someone is hungry. Let's go get you some food."

We walk arm in arm back to the living room.

~Trinity~

I smell the food first and my stomach growls again. Dee looks to me with a smile. "Come on in here, Trin. Oh, sorry. Is it okay if I call you Trin?" I shake my head yes as she finishes, "I made you something to eat so let's get you over here and fix you a plate." Everyone watches me as I walk up to the breakfast bar and take a seat. I don't even care that they are watching me, I begin to devour the food like this is my first meal in days, because really it is.

Des clears his throat. "Honey, we need to talk while you eat, is that okay with you?" I nod and stuff more eggs into my mouth as he goes on, "We've been discussing what the next steps are for you. For now, we need to keep your location secret, so your father doesn't cause any trouble."

At the mention of that man, I drop my fork, losing my appetite immediately, and hug myself tightly, trying to find that place in my mind where he doesn't exist. Dee and Fern both hug me from each side, trying to give me some comfort where there is none to be had. I go through my routine in my mind, blocking any thoughts of him out. Once I take some time to regain some of my composure, I look up to see Des standing on the other side of the island with another man. "Trinity, do you remember Wolf?"

I look at the huge man then back to Des. "He works for you, doesn't he?"

"Yes, he does, honey, and he also lives about ten minutes from here on a secluded ranch. I think this is the best place for you to take some time and heal."

"Both Fern and I will visit you all the time," Dee Dee says. "Wolf has dogs, cats, and even horses. It's so quiet and relaxing where he lives, and we think it will help give you some much-needed time to concentrate on getting you and the baby healthy. You need time and a place to recover physically and emotionally."

Wolf walks up to me, putting his hand on my

shoulder. "My name is Wolf Youngblood, little one. I want to let you know that you will always be safe with me. I will protect you as if you were my sister, my own flesh and blood. I want you to find serenity for yourself and that baby, and most importantly, feel safe. This is something you not only need, but also deserve, so please let my home be a place of peace for you as long as you need it."

"Whatever you all think is best. I can never begin to repay you for what you've done for me tonight, even if it was done for Cadence and not for me. I've never had support from anyone because I've never wanted anyone to know. I need you all to know that I didn't stay because I had nowhere else to go or because I didn't want to leave. I tried to leave once but my father knows a lot of bad people, so when they found me and brought me back to him, he beat me for days, and not just a few. He made sure I knew what would happen if I ever tried to leave him again. After that, I was too afraid to try."

After I speak, the room is suddenly quiet, and I can feel the angry vibe from everyone in the room.

"I hope you don't mind me asking you this, honey, but how long has this been going on? How long has he been abusing you?" Des asks the question, but it almost sounds like he doesn't really want to know the answer.

"It's gone on for a really long time. My mom left when I was five. I think it was because she couldn't handle his abuse any longer, so once she left, he took his anger out on me. He made sure I got the physical and emotional brunt of his anger, especially the more he drank. People saw what was happening, but no one, not even the people from my church or the school I attended tried to help me." I don't know if I should go on with this story. I'm in front of people I don't even know, but they saved me tonight, and telling them what I've just told them has felt like a boulder is starting to lift from my chest. I feel as if I've gone this far in telling them of my father, I should tell them the whole story. I feel safe enough to do that with these people. "On my thirteenth birthday, he showed me what real hell truly was as he beat me for accepting a gift, just a small flower from a boy at school. That was the night that he sexually assaulted me, for use of a better word. He told me that I should get to see what that boy wanted from me and he should be the one to show me, and if I ever told anyone, they would all call me a nasty, dirty whore."

I feel terrible about what I just told them because now they are all looking at me stunned, especially Cadence. Instead of breaking down, I calmly tell Des, "My father, Roman, is a lunatic and he will not take this lying down, I can promise you that. Like I said before, he has some really bad friends too, so please be careful. I would feel horrible if anything happened to any of you for saving me."

Without knowing what else to do, I let them all gawk at me while I lift my fork back up and try to seem calm while I finished eating my meal. I hear Dee Dee and Fern quietly crying next to me, but I continue on with my eating, waiting for this moment to pass.

Finally, Des clears his throat and grabs the girls, pulling them away, seeing that I need a little bit of space right now.

As everyone starts to leave me in peace, Cadence remains standing there, looking at me like he's never seen me before. "It's kind of funny to me, Cadence, that you're still standing here. My dad may have broken me, but you had to come along and just crush what was left of my heart and soul. My dad was proven right by what you did to me. That that was what boys wanted from me. I heard the rumors about you, but I wanted so much to believe you because we were friends, and I thought I could trust you but you made me believe a lie. I'm so naïve and gullible, right, Cadence? Is that what made you target me?" He starts to speak but I continue, "I have never been able to choose anything for myself. All my choices and decisions have always been taken from me, but then I made a decision, and I chose you, but you didn't choose me. You, just like him, made me feel worthless and cheap. I have no more trust to give to any man because the two men that I should have been able to trust, and depend on the most, have both taken that away from me too."

"You can't compare me to him, Trinity. I fucked things up between us, but you can't blame me for all this."

"You didn't even have the decency to tell me about the condom ripping. If Des hadn't said something to me, I would have been completely lost. You never even thought twice about me after I left your shop. You humiliated me in front of everyone. You continued on with your loose women, not once thinking of what hell I was going through, waiting to find out if I was pregnant, and what my dad would do to me when he found out. I appreciate what you have done for my baby and me tonight, but just like I said, this is my baby. You will have nothing to do with my child until I see you grow some fucking balls and start being a real man and not a whore. Are we clear?"

You could have heard a pin drop it got so quiet in the house. Cadence looks down at me, responding quietly, yet menacingly, "First, before I go any further with what you just shared, I have to ask you if this is my kid. Call me a dick for asking, but if you weren't on the pill when we were together, how do I know this isn't his kid?"

As the men and women in the room gasp at Cadence's insulting question, I see his reason for asking it, but how dare he think that I would sit here all night and not tell him if he wasn't the father. "It sickens me right now just to think it could ever be either of yours, but he hasn't forced himself on me for years because the asshole can't get it up anymore. That's why he beats me twice as bad as he used to, so just to clear this up for your simple-minded ass, yes, Cadence. You ARE the sperm donor."

"Trinity, you know nothing about me and that's on me, but listen closely. I don't care what you say; no one is keeping me from my kid, not even its mother. You had a shit life? Well so did I, but that's a story for another time. This is *my* family that is willing to help you out, and they make me proud to know each and every one of them. You will not shut me out, so you better get that through your head right now."

"Then I'll just say goodbye to *your* family, and I will be on my way. I don't want to be here because you deem it so. There is no way in hell you will ever tell me what I will and won't do regarding my child, so kiss my ass and move out of my way."

CHAPTER FIFTEEN

DES

I look between Trinity and Cadence, knowing this is going nowhere fast. Before they continue to argue all night, I look to Wolf, who nods his head.

Wolf steps forward, lightly touching Trinity's arm. "There's no need to go anywhere, little one. I made you a promise and I intend to keep that promise. Are you ready to go? We need to get you home so you can get some much-needed rest."

Cadence glares at Wolf but says nothing. Trinity looks up at Wolf and says, "No disrespect, Wolf, but can I trust a mammoth-sized Native American?"

At her comment, the tension eases within the room. I laugh, looking her in the eye. "Honey, I would trust him with my own life with no second thought, so yes. You can trust this mammoth-sized man." Everyone else starts to chime in, but what Dee says grabs Trinity's attention.

"Trin, I would trust Wolf with both of my kids, and

for the record, we are here not only for Cadence, but also you. Don't forget that."

"You have kids?"

"Yes, honey. I have two; my daughter's name is Daisy and my son's name is Jagger. They aren't much younger than you... actually, how old are you?"

"I'm twenty-two, Dee Dee."

Dee throws her head back laughing then looks at Fern. "Oh hell, Fern. To be twenty-two again, and Trin, call me Dee. Damn, those were the days, weren't they?"

Fern smiles and replies, "Yes they were, Dee."

I see Trinity quietly watching the interaction between Dee and Fern like she's never seen anything like it before in her young life. The love and friendship between those two ladies is a sight to see.

Both women walk over to Trinity and pull her into a tight hug while Dee looks down at her with a motherly gaze. "Honey, you are now part of all of this good, bad, and ugly, so you are going to need to get used to it."

Some of the men are speaking about heading to a bar in town while the women gather all of Trinity's scarce belongings. As her things are put into the back seat, Wolf walks her to the passenger side, opening the door and looking down at her with a smile. "Once we get you to the ranch, I want you to make yourself at home, okay?" She shakes her head and slowly makes her way into the truck.

~Cadence~

Watching the interaction between Trinity and Wolf from the back of my truck, I feel like my blood is boiling in my body. I start to walk toward the two people I want to address. I'm pissed off at the circumstances and the way everything's turning out. Wolf observes me approaching, seeing my emotions running across my face. He helps Trinity into the truck, telling her to put her seat belt on and closes the door. He meets me halfway down his extra-long truck bed, where we stare at each other for what feels like hours not minutes, when Wolf puts his arm around my shoulders and walks to the end of the truck. "Little brother, you need to stop with this jealousy you are feeling toward me because I'm doing this for you. You know me, Cadence —known me for years—and I'm offended that you would think I would step on your toes for a woman who's in pain and hurting. You don't see this, but she needs a friend and someone to feel safe with, and I'm trying to provide that to her for you." I look up at the huge man who is looking down at me. "We may not know everything about each other, kid, but never would I risk a friendship by going down that road." Looking into Wolf's eyes, I see that he means every word and I start to feel my eyes filling up with tears. Fuck. The last thing I need to do is fucking cry in front of Wolf. Just as

I start to pull away and head back to my truck, Wolf pulls me into his broad chest.

"Listen, Cadence. We all have shit in our past and we all make mistakes. What makes a man a man is if he can learn from his mistakes and become a better person. I don't know your past, but I can see you're hurting, so I want you to remember that I'm always going to have your back, no matter what it is, okay?"

I feel the warmth on my cheeks and can't seem to find my voice, so I nod my head. Wolf continues, "Des has always given us room to become who we're supposed to be; no pressure or questions, so I'm going to do the same for you. My home is always open to you, as you are part of my family, but I'll not allow you to hurt that innocent girl sitting in my truck, brother. Figure your shit out before you try to bury it all on her shoulders. She's fighting her own battle of shit and I don't know which is worse, but you two have a lot to deal with together and apart, not to mention a baby on the way. Talk to Fern and Doc if you have to, but once again, brother, figure your shit out. You have no right to tell her what she can and cannot do. She's been going through this for months, all alone, while you're out getting your dick wet and living it up without a care in the world. Don't blame her for the way she feels, she is entitled to it. So let her have it and you take it when she dishes it. It's what a man does."

I wipe my face, trying to steady my shaking hands. "You're right, I am fucked up. I've known it for a long time but I haven't done anything to make it right. I can't let it continue, not with a kid on the way and Trinity needing support, not stress. I've made her hate me, so now I need to prove to her that I will stand by her and be supportive to her in any way that she will let me." I look toward the cab of his truck. "Can I have a minute with her, Wolf, please?"

Wolf grins. "I'm going to head back in and get me a bottle of water for the road."

I approach the driver side door, open it, and climb up behind the wheel. Trinity looks my way with a smile until she sees it's me then her smile disappears. I know I deserve her attitude, but her actions still hurt. "Trinity, I owe you a huge fucking apology." She just stares at me, not saying a word. "I owe you more than an apology, and soon I'd like to explain some things about me to you, but right now, please know that I am here for both you and our baby. I won't make excuses and insult you with why I didn't man up and do the shit I should have done for you, but I truly don't want you to go through this alone. Please know that from this moment on, you can depend on me."

Trinity continues to look at me for a long time, and then she finally speaks, "Have you forgotten that I've listened to your pretty words before? Look where that has gotten me—where it has gotten us. I can't sit here and tell you what you want to hear. Your words have no value to me and you've proven that to me without blinking an eye. I think you believe what you're saying to me at this moment, but I've always said actions speak louder than words. You have a lot to show me,

Cadence. I'm not talking about for me, because whatever we had is done, but this baby doesn't deserve to have a father who only wants to be there when it's convenient for him. I can't make you promises that I can't keep until I see something different in you."

My head jerks up. "What does that mean, Trinity?"

"It means that I'm not going to push you away from our baby if your actions show that you mean what you say, that's all, Cadence."

Before I can reply, the driver side door opens, and Wolf touches my arm. "Brother, enough for tonight. Both Trinity and the baby need some rest and it's going to take some time once we get to my house to set her up in the spare room. The sooner we start, the sooner she can get some much-needed rest and feel safe."

I look at Trinity and see the sincerity reflected in her eyes. "I won't let you down again, sweetie. I swear to you." I reach over and grab her hand, giving it a gentle squeeze and then I look to her belly. She places my hand on her belly without me having to ask. I start rubbing it softly as I say, "Not gonna let you down again either, Tiny." I give her a huge smile before I climb down out of the truck as Wolf waits to take my place behind the wheel.

"So did you learn anything?" Wolf asks with a grin on his face.

"Wolf, actions speak louder than words, dude. Don't you know that?" As I walk away from the truck, I can hear Trinity giggling softly.

CHAPTER SIXTEEN

WOLF

As I pull down the dirt access road to my home, I glance at Trinity who is curled up in the passenger seat, fast asleep. Her head is resting on her cupped hands with her forehead resting on the cool glass window of the door. I slow down so I don't rock the truck with all the uneven gravel we are quickly approaching; I don't want to jar the little girl any more than she already has been. My temper rises as I glance back at her, or more specifically, her battered face. God, I would like five fucking minutes with her asshole father—no, scratch that—he is not a father because if he were, Trinity would not be black and blue. As my thoughts turn dark, I hear her start to whimper. I reach over and lightly rub her leg to try and comfort her. Immediately her eyes open and stare at my hand on her upper thigh. I immediately remove my hand, softly whispering, "Little one, you're having some sort of nightmare. I was just trying to comfort you, nothing more." Her eyes move from her thigh to look directly into my eyes. To me, it feels like she is staring straight into my soul as she seems to look at me forever, but after a minute or two, she nods and straightens up in the seat, lightly moaning. "What's the matter?" I ask.

"I'm just stiff and really sore, that's all. I would kill to soak in a tub for hours."

At her comment I look her way and say with laughter in my voice. "Your wish is my command, little one. I have a claw-foot tub in my house so you can soak for however long you want."

My breath catches in my throat as she looks at me with an angelic smile on her face. "Really? You have a huge tub? Can I please use it? Please?"

God, Cadence, you are such an idiot, I instantly think. "Of course, you can, Trinity. You can use anything in my house that you want. I ask that for as long as you are here that you consider it your home, also. By the way, is it okay to sit in a hot bath while pregnant?"

"Do you have internet at your home? I can look it up."

"Great idea," I reply as I stop in front of my home. As she turns her head, I hear her gasp and see her smile. I worked very hard on my home, and I know it is breathtaking. It is an L-shaped, raised ranch made with logs and stonework. Trinity sits quietly, just staring at the house. "You okay, honey?"

She shakes her head then looks over her shoulder. "I can't believe I'll be staying here. It's like a piece of heaven. Never before have I slept, let alone lived, in a place like this."

I turn off the truck and jump out, walking around to open Trinity's door. I reach up to help her down but as she moves to get out, she starts to fall. Grabbing on to her before she lands, I grab around her ribs, not thinking. I'm just trying to stop her fall when she cries out loudly. As soon as she's on her feet, I move my hands to her shoulders to help steady her. She's biting her bottom lip as tears appear in her eyes, but then I see her eyes start to roll and I know that she's about to pass out. "Shit" is all I get out before she goes totally limp in my arms and I'm trying to gently hold on to her dead weight. Fuck!!!!

I lift her up and approach my front deck, placing her on a wicker lounger so I can reach for my phone. I dial Doc's number and wait patiently until Fern answers the phone. "Fern, sweetie, I need Doc if you can spare him. Trinity passed out and I have her lying on my lounger by the front door. I don't know what to do, but what I do know that it seems she is breathing okay. Not sure if this has anything to do with the beatings though." I hear Fern speaking to someone and then I hear two male voices, one trying to calm the other one down. Shit. Cadence is there and now he's freaking out. Oh well. He would have found out one way or another. While Doc tries to calm the kid down, I ask Fern to put Cadence on the phone.

"What the fuck, Wolf? She hasn't even been with

you for ten minutes and something goes wrong? We're on our way, shit for brains."

I take a deep breath, knowing that when Cadence feels scared he puts up his tough asshole guy act. I clear my throat and tell Cadence, "You need to calm your shit down, kid. Fern doesn't need to see you like this, especially right now. You hear me?" Immediately I hear Cadence take a few deep, calming breaths before I hear him tell Fern that he's sorry and hangs up the phone. This is just great. More drama is not what I need any more tonight, nor does Trinity.

I unlock and open the front door up wide, then I gently pick Trinity up carrying her to an oversized chair just as she starts to come to. "What happened?"

I push her hair off of her face and tell her, "You passed out. I don't want you to move until Doc gets here to check you out." She nods her head as her eyes start to close. "Try and stay awake, Trin. I don't need you passing out on me again."

Her eyes open and she giggles. "You're the second person who has called me 'Trin' tonight. I like the way it sounds."

"More than 'little one'?" I ask with a smile.

"No, I like them both."

We both sit in silence for a short while until we hear a door slam and heavy footsteps running up the stairs. The front door is thrown open and Cadence stands there, breathing heavily. "Are you okay, Trinity?" She looks at him for just a moment and then busts out in laughter. Cadence looks like the devil himself with his hair ruffled by his hands and his eyes are pitch-black and spitting fire at me.

As he continues to stare between Trinity and me, Doc comes in and sits next to her. "Trinity, can you tell me if anything hurts? Do you remember what happened?"

She shakes her head and groans, "No, Doc. All I remember is losing my balance getting out of the truck and when Wolf caught me before falling, he pushed in on my side. I had immediate pain, and then became nauseous and dizzy."

Doc takes a light from his pocket and checks her eyes. As he moves it around, Trinity starts to sway and moan while grabbing her head. Doc puts the light down and gently takes her wrist in his hand and checks her pulse. As everyone watches, Doc checks her glands in her neck and moves her head from side to side. Trinity closes her eyes and looks again like she minutes from passing out again.

Doc looks in my direction and asks, "Do you have some ginger ale or seltzer water?" I nod my head yes turning and go toward the kitchen. I hear Cadence and Fern step closer to Doc as Fern asks, "Gabriel, what do you think it is?" I listen for his answer as I get some things together from the kitchen. "I'm not sure, but I'm thinking Trinity either has an inner ear infection, or maybe even a slightly punctured eardrum. We need to get her seen by a specialist ASAP. Kid, would you mind sitting her up, in case she needs to throw up? I'll go find a bucket to keep close."

I'm already walking out of the kitchen when I hear Doc. So I grab a bucket and make my way back into the living room, carrying the bucket and also a tray with some ginger ale, oyster crackers, and saltines. I place everything on the coffee table and reach toward Trinity as Cadence growls. I immediately step back with a smirk on my face, but then I turn and give Doc a serious look. "How's the little one doin'?" He tells me again what I've already heard from the kitchen but continues to give me more information. "She is beyond exhausted and just spent. She's underweight, beaten, bruised, and I'm pretty sure her ribs are badly bruised, possibly even broken. They will have to heal on their own because it's not good for the healing process to wrap them up. Let's get her hydrated and then off to bed. She'll have to deal with everything else in the morning, possibly finding doctors farther out of town so her father doesn't get any idea of where she is." Doc goes to stand by Fern. He grabs her hand and kisses her forehead.

We all watch as Cadence gets Trinity to drink her ginger ale and coax her into eating a few crackers. Once the soda is gone, Cadence asks if he can help get Trinity to bed. No one is sure of whom he is asking, so no one says anything, waiting on Trinity to reply. She doesn't say anything, but she takes his hand in hers and tells him that would be fine. Cadence immediately gets to his feet and pulls her up from the oversized chair.

Trinity thanks both Doc and Fern while promising them both she'll look tomorrow for a physician who is not local and make an appointment. She releases

Cadence's hand and walks to me, hugging me around my middle, her head barely reaching my chest. "Thank you, Wolf, for all that you've done for me tonight. You'll never know what it means to me that you opened your home to me, a stranger, and for once in my miserable life, given me a safe haven. Oh, and also for not freaking when I passed out. You are my newest friend, and my hero."

The room is so quiet you can hear a pin drop as I grab her hands from around me and hold them in mine. "Little one, there is no need to thank me for anything. It makes me very happy that you feel you can trust me and feel safe in my home. I want you to sleep well tonight and know that nothing will harm you here, and we' get right on top of looking into these doctor's appointments tomorrow after you've had a chance to rest." Turning her toward Cadence, I tell him, "Help her get settled. Take her to the second bedroom down the hall, on the left. I just put clean bedding down last week so it's all ready for her. There's an extra toothbrush under the cabinet in the bathroom down the hall and she can unpack her stuff tomorrow. I'll get her a T-shirt to sleep in." Cadence just nods his head in agreement then heads down the hall with Trinity in his arms.

CHAPTER SEVENTEEN

TRINITY

The next day, actually, closer to evening since I've practically slept the day away, I'm standing in the bathroom looking at myself in the mirror, totally shocked and appalled at my appearance. My hands continually rise to touch my face as I bounce from foot to foot. The bruising on any visible skin is a dark purple and blue. My father really did a job on me this time, and the amount of alcohol he consumed didn't help at all. As these thoughts start to run through my mind, I start to think what could have happened if Cadence and his friends hadn't come and gotten me out of there when they did. His attitude was getting worse every day and because I didn't want to involve anyone in my shit, I didn't seek out the help that was offered to me. I've come so close to losing my baby. It wasn't bad in the beginning. I didn't go anywhere; I worked and came home, cleaned, and made dinner. It wasn't until I started getting morning sickness, then he found a pregnancy test that I thought I had hidden deep in the garbage bag, but of course the bag broke when I was taking it out, and with my shitty luck, that's what he saw. How unbelievable is that?

I start shaking as tears run down my cheeks. I could have lost my baby before it was even born because I was too afraid to stand up to the sadistic bastard who happens to be not only my abuser but also my father.

I jump as someone knocks on the bathroom door. "Baby, you okay in there?" Cadence asks tentatively. I'm so overcome with emotion that I can't even find my voice to answer him back.

After a couple of minutes, he tries again, "Trinity, please tell me that you're okay. If you don't answer me, I'm coming in, babe."

I try to get the words out, but it feels like my jaw is locked shut. I can feel his impatience as he starts to mutter under his breath. Then I watch—as if in slow motion—while the bathroom door starts to open, and by the time I see his face, I'm an absolute wreck and begin crying so loudly that I don't even hear anyone coming into the bathroom. I'm so lost in my mess that I don't realize Cadence has picked me up and carried me to the bed. "Baby, whatever it is, it's going to be okay. I can't leave you in the shitter for five minutes alone, can I?" Cadence's choice of words for the bathroom brings me out of my head and forces me to giggle, followed by a very loud snort.

Taking both hands, I put them into my shirt and up to my face to wipe the tears and snot from my cheeks while all three men, along with Fern, watch quietly as I try to pull myself together.

The doorbell rings, scaring the shit out of everyone, and Wolf leaves to check it out. Minutes later, he returns with Des behind him, worry apparent in his eyes.

Glancing around the room, I take everyone in and feel the need to say to all of them. "I'm so sorry to be such a burden on all of you. It finally hit me in the bathroom, that if you hadn't gotten me out of that trailer last night, my dad would have probably killed not only me but also my baby. It was so stupid of me to not reach out to you, Des, or even you, Cadence, for help. I should have called the police, but after no one bothered to help me when I reached out before, and with his friends, I didn't feel like I had any other choice but to accept it until I could find a permanent way out."

The feeling in the room is suddenly awkward as Doc, Fern, and Des tense while Wolf glances in Cadence's direction. When I look his way, I'm shocked to see that his cheeks are wet. I immediately look toward the three other men in the room to see uncertainty in their expressions. Fern turns and leaves the room, her shoulders hunched over as if in defeat.

A throat clears and I move my gaze back to Cadence. "Baby, do you mind if I sit next to you? I need to tell you something?"

"Do you want us to leave, Cadence?" asks Doc.

Cadence shakes his head no, telling Doc, "You might as well hear what I have to say. It's been a long time coming, Doc, and you know most of it anyway. Please, guys, if you don't mind plant your asses down. I have something to share with Trinity and it should be shared with you. Shame and pride have kept me quiet for years from letting y'all in, but it's time for me to let this shit go, or at least start the process. I want that to begin with all of you, my family."

Everyone finds a place in the room to sit, ready to hear what it's that Cadence has to say. We give him time to think of what he's about to reveal while he sits next to me, gripping my hand like it's an anchor. He's nervous so I close my fingers around his hand, letting him know that I'm here. "We're all here for you, and no matter what you tell us, we won't judge you. Look at what you know now about my situation. Nothing could be as bad as that, can it?"

"Trinity, first and foremost, I owe you an apology for how this all turned out. I was a huge dick not to mention a total asshole to you, but never intended to take advantage of you or treat you like shit which is exactly what I did. I'm not going to use my past as an excuse, but since that time in my life, I've tried to escape my nightmares and insecurities by using sex as a way to avoid what truly has been bottled up and bothering me. Never in all these years have I sat down and truly dealt with what had happened to me, and because of that, my selfishness and lack of having dealt with the situation caused me to use you and make you suffer. I never intended to hurt or humiliate you, Trinity. I really wanted to, for the first time in my life, begin a real, meaningful relationship with you whatever that even means. But that day in Des' office I just freaked out and dealt with you the only way I knew how, and that was by acting like I didn't give a shit and to get the hell outta there because I was scared a feeling that I hate."

I watch Cadence look to Doc, who gives him a nod of support to continue. "You need to know this, Trinity, because you're not alone. I know exactly how you feel in regarding being abused and suffering at the hands of your dad because—" He clears his throat and looks down at his feet. "When I was a kid, I never thought bad things could ever happen to my family until my old man took off one day, never showing his face again. And to this day, I have no idea why. I was probably five while Griffin, my baby brother, was two years old. Ryker, my older brother, was eight. After Dad left, it was a struggle for all of us, our mom especially, but we always pushed forward. After a couple of years, Mom started datin'. Some dudes we liked, while others, not so much. One day Mom came home with this bear of a man and told us boys that the two of them were in love and getting married. She said he would be our new dad. None of us boys were happy with her choice, as we all, at one time or another since he been coming around, had run-ins with Duke. But we wanted our mom to be happy, so we tried really hard to make it work for Mom's sake.

"There were bumps in the road in the beginning, but everyone was trying, then Duke lost his job and spent his days on the couch, drinking, while Mom worked two jobs to make ends meet. Ryker even got a paper route to help, and still Duke did nothing but drink beer and hang out with his loser friends always at our house eating and drinking.

"I started to see a difference in my mom first. She was always so affectionate, always hugging and kissing us, always showing her love for us, but over time she started to distance herself from us, her boys as she always called us. She stopped being warm and tender and even when she tried, it just wasn't with the same devotion she always showed. Funny how a kid would notice that, but being that we had it for so long, once it's being taken away, you totally miss it. We certainly did especially not knowin' what we did to make it go away.

"She started to wear long-sleeved tops, even when it was warm out. Once Griffin was goofin' around and turned, grabbing Mom's arm and she let out a scream. Ryker pushed her sleeve up to reveal some huge bruises up and down her arm. When we asked her what happened, she told us she fell into the wall vacuuming, or some shit. Then Griffin started acting strange. He withdrew from Ryker, Mom, and me completely and seemed to always hanging with Duke, day in and day out. They would spend hours in Griffin's room, mostly while Mom was at work. When we said something to her about it, she confronted them, but they both said they were just finding things to do together as father and son. One day after Ryker and I got home from school, earlier than usual, we heard Griffin crying, screaming, and begging for something to stop. We ran down the hall and found Duke raping my little brother. I will never forget that sight of my brother being held down by a man twice his size, being forced to endure something so vile and disgusting by a man who was playacting to be our dad but was nothing but a sick motherfucker. By this time Ryker was a teenager. He was built since he was lifting weights, so he got Duke off Grif and beat the livin' shit out of him.

"Everything seemed to happen so fast from that point. By the time our mom rushed home, the cops along with an ambulance were there. I have no idea who called them. Grif was in bad shape. Apparently, it had been going on for a while, and do you want to know why he didn't tell anyone? Duke the asshole that he is threated to do it to us, so Grif thought he could take it and no one else would have to get hurt like him.

"Duke was long gone the pussy he was. For some reason he was let go and didn't want to face the music so the cops started lookin' for him when mom and Griffin filed charges, but that was all they could do. Our hands were tied cause he was in the wind. We thought that would be the last we would ever hear from that sick bastard thinkin' he was out of our lives, so we tried to move on, struggling to find our way back to some kind of normal family for us, especially for my little brother Griffin. It took him some time to heal, not only physically, but also mentally. Mom on advice from the doctors and police took him to talk to a rape counselor so he could get it out and after about ten months, everything was going good. Mom was getting back to her old self, while Griffin was slowly coming back around. It was a really rough year for him with all the psychological shit going on in his mind, but he was coming back to us. Then in one day, things changed us again, but this time for Ryker.

"Grif, Mom, and I were playing some stupid board game in the kitchen when we heard very loud noises from the wooded area out behind our backyard. Didn't know what it was but we all rushed out to find Ryker beaten to a pulp."

I take in a shocked breath, looking to see that everyone in the room is staring at Cadence with tears in their eyes.

"Ryker told us that Duke did it as payback for Ryker beating his ass, but Duke wasn't alone, or Ryker wouldn't have had a problem fighting him off. Duke was a huge ass bear, but he was weakling. So he had help. The thing that we all knew, but Ryker would never say, was that Duke also raped him that day. This put our family back to square one, always looking over our shoulders, bringing back past suffering along with huge amounts of new emotions and pain as well. Ryker was never the same, so a few months after it happened, he turned eighteen and immediately joined the service; the Marines. It was his only way to deal with what happened. Ryker told us on the day he shipped out that no one would ever hurt him again. He was gonna make sure of it by being trained by the best. Mom got a restraining order and for a while we were very careful, but after a few more years, time went on and we let our guards down again, and I became his next target.

"I don't know how it happened, but somehow Duke found me and kidnapped me. I was at a bar with a friend drinkin' one night, and the next thing I remember was waking up in some shitty cabin out in the middle of nowhere, tied to a bed frame. Asshole somehow drugged my drink and brought me out there where he beat on me for days, making me so weak couldn't get away even if he gave me a chance which he didn't. There were a few times that he would leave for a day or two, leaving me with no food or water. I had to piss myself cause I couldn't get up being cuffed and left bleeding on that bed until one day he came back, finally makin' his move."

Wolf leaves then returns with beers and a glass of water for me and hands them out to everyone. Cadence takes a deep breath, reaches for first for his water gulping it down then grabs beer slugging that off quickly.

"So, Trinity, I kind of have an idea of how you feel because that night changed my life, and I've never been the same since. I was seventeen when Duke raped me. He raped me repeatedly that day until I passed out from the intense pain. I woke to more of the same and don't remember much except that there were times I asked— no I begged him to put me out of my misery-to let me die. He obviously didn't give me that, but he did something much worse. He brought in his friends for a special party, and along with Duke, they all did things to me—made me do things to them that were so beyond fucked up. Some of those memories still haunt me to this day."

He wipes his eyes but continues. I can see that he's trying to get it out as fast as he can because he may not finish if he has a chance to break down.

"What has fucked with me more than anything since that time is that through all the sick-ass shit that happened in that room, my body seemed to fail me cause it liked it. They would work me and work me over and over until they made me come, then I would come again, and again. How the fuck could my own body betray me that way?"

The disgust in his voice pulls me from my thoughts. I feel what he's feeling right now. I know what he means, so I squeeze his shoulder to get his attention. "You're wrong, Cadence. That was just a body function reacting to stimulation. We may not have wanted it, but it's normal and that's the truth. There were times when I was being abused that my body reacted since my '*dad*' made it his mission to learn how to make me respond. Not me, but my body. He took a sadistic pleasure in knowing that he was making my body react to him, even though my mind was shutting down and somewhere else. Don't you dare feel wrong or sick about it. You never stood a chance against a pack of rabid degenerates who were making it their mission to do that kind of damage to you."

Wolf stands and walks to Cadence and tells him, "Listen to the little one, Cadence. She's right. No matter what, you had no control over what happened to you, and you should never hold your head in shame because there's nothing to be ashamed of. Those men will face their punishment one way or another, as I truly believe that what goes around, comes around eventually. Everyone here is your family and there's nothing you could say or do that could ever change that. Don't you ever forget it." Cadence grabs Wolf's hand off his shoulder and gives it a fist bump.

Then turning to me, he finishes up, "We have each suffered torture and abuse throughout our lives by men we trusted who don't deserve to breathe the same air as we do, but it's on us, to make the most out of our lives and not let our abusers win. That's how we beat them. Please, Trinity. We can be one another's support. Besides Doc, Fern, and some parts to a counselor, I have never told anyone that story of my past. Des found me and still I never told him the story until tonight."

Des looks like he could tear the dry wall off the studs with his bare hands. The quiet in the room is overwhelming until Doc suggests, "That's enough for tonight. Everyone needs to get some rest, especially Trinity." He then gets up, heading toward the door. "I'm a phone call away if you need me. I've got to get Fern home."

Wolf begins to pick up the empty bottles and glasses. Des approaches Cadence, reaching out and pulling him in tight. "I'm so fuckin' proud of you for what you did tonight. Never forget how strong you really are. You're a survivor." Cadence lets out a long breath and softly thanks Des. Des looks at me and then back at Cadence. "You both need to get some sleep. You know where I'm at if either of you need anything." Turning, he walks out of the room behind Wolf, softly shutting the door behind him.

I know that Cadence is aware of me staring up at him, but he can't seem to look at me. Finally, I bump his shoulder, asking him if he would spend the night with me. Looking shocked to his core, I explain what I'm asking, "I've been having really bad nightmares and when I wake up, it seems like I'm still trapped in said night terrors before my head clears. After what you just shared with everyone tonight, I just need to try and make me feel like I'm not all alone, so I figured we could comfort each other. No hanky-panky, Cadence, and I mean that. I don't want to hate or be mad at you because no matter how badly you treated me, we were friends before all of this, so why don't we try going back to that, before we did the '*nasty*.'"

Cadence lets out a chuckle. "I still have nightmares too, Trinity. I'd like to stay with you too."

I feel like a heavy weight lift off my heart. I really don't want to hold on to this bitterness and resentment toward Cadence. I want us to be able to find a commonality between us so that we can raise this baby together without the unnecessary baggage. That won't do our kid any good. We need to get in a good space with each other for the sake of our baby.

~Cadence~

As I lie in bed listenin' to the soft sounds coming from Trinity, I think about the last couple of hours. I can't believe how relieved and almost peaceful I feel like a weight has been lifted. Never not once since my time with Duke had I felt any type of calm in my life. With my hands behind my head, I think about Trinity and our little baby. I don't know what it's about her, but she calms the voices in my head and helps with the pain that's been a constant in my life for so many years. When I glance at her, I think to myself, *I've been with prettier, sexier, and much more experienced girls than her, but no one has ever come close to touchin' that place in my heart the way she has.* I'm not good with emotions and feelings toward other people, except my family, and I'm not even that good with those. She's new territory for me. Trinity, in her own way, was always tryin' to see the good guy in me, but I blew that all to hell.

Suddenly Trinity rolls over, throwing her arm around my waist and holds on tight, moving her leg just over mine, causing my cock to stand up and take notice. I let out a moan and try to shift away, but her hand at my waist tightens even more, trappin' me in place. I pull my hands from behind my head and gently grab her shoulders to move her off me but I hear her whisper, just barely, "No, Cadence. Please don't leave me. We need you."

I stop immediately and hold my breath. What? Is she fuckin' with me? *They* need me? Who are *they*? Then it suddenly hits me like a punch to the gut. She's dreaming about me leavin' her and our baby, and it's then that I feel something break open in my chest. It's a tingling that starts in the center of my chest and spreads, fillin' that part of my heart that has been dead for so long. I blink uncontrollably as I feel the wet flowing from my eyes, down my cheeks. I've two people who need me now and I want it—I want it so badly I can taste it. This feelin' is more satisfying than any pill or piece of pussy I could ever have. It's pure-perfection-untraveled ground. As we sleep, I have no nightmares, I dream of nothin'. Pure peace of mind for once in my life.

CHAPTER EIGHTEEN

CADENCE

As I put the oil plug back into the car I'm workin' on, I think about the last couple of weeks. After the night Trinity and I revealed our pasts to one another along with my whole family, things seem to have calmed down and we're making progress in our newfound friendship. She's still livin' at Wolf's, which I've come to accept. It really is the safest place for her to be right now. No one would even consider messing with Wolf.

Her ribs are healing nicely, according to Doc, and the bruises all over her body are just about gone. With her having regular meals and plenty of sleep, she is lookin' better and better each and every day. Pregnancy is finally agreeing with her. The morning sickness has stopped, and her body is definitely changing for sure. Her tits are fuller, as well as her hips. The small swell of her belly catches my eye constantly, always making my heart race. My baby is growin' in there, and the male part of me just wants to go around and pound on my chest, but also that same part of me also sees these changes to her body, causing me to have a constant hard-on.

A couple of days ago I caught her dancing in Wolf's kitchen while cooking. I watched as her hips swayed from side to side and felt my cock pitching a tent in my cargo pants. As I went to adjust myself, she turned and caught me. Looking disappointed, she rolled her eyes and shook her head. Yesterday she was playing with Spirit, one of Wolf's rescue dogs. She was on all fours just like the dog, playin' with him, shoving a toy around the floor when again, I got hard. Before she could catch me, I walked away from her with a loud groan, but I didn't get away as unnoticed as I thought as I heard her giggling, and it sure the fuck wasn't at Spirit.

With everything on my plate, work, the upcoming Charity Ride for Fern, and now Trinity, I thought I'd be stressed out, but it's exactly the opposite. I feel like I've a purpose in my life now. Every night after work I go straight up to my place, feed my kittens, clean their litter boxes, and spend some time with them. As silly as it sounds, the kittens give me a purpose I never had in my life before. They depend on me for everything, and that makes me feel like I'm not only needed but necessary for their lives. After my time with the kittens, I then head to Wolf's for dinner, and to spend the night with Trinity.

I have a new respect for Wolf. I had no friggin' idea of all that was on Wolf's plate. Besides the garage and his fabrication skills, Wolf has a full-time functioning ranch/farm, not sure which is the correct term, but besides a few cows, a couple of pigs, a chicken coop, and the horse corrals, there are also the rescues that are free to run his property. By property, I mean acre after acre of God's pure untouched land. Over the years Wolf has expanded his acreage and until now, I had no idea why a guy his age would need so much land, but now I'm clued into the reason.

In the far back, behind the main house, are little cottages scattered here and there. At first glance I counted nine, but there could be more. I asked Wolf why they are there, and instead of tellin' me, he asks me to walk with him. We walk toward the cabins and as we get closer, I can hear voices in conversation and laughter. When we pass by the tree line, I'm shocked at what I see.

There are different sized families out, either by one of the cabins or hangin' around visiting and barbecuing. Kids are playing ball or sitting at picnic benches that are scattered around. A young girl, no more than probably I her early to mid-twenties, sits on a lawn chair with a Kindle on her lap, reading.

When I look her way, I pull in a deep breath as I feel my anger spread throughout my body. Her face looks like someone used it for a punching bag. Worse than Trinity's did a while back. Wolf pushes me in her direction, and I notice that she starts to tremble as we approach her. Wolf squats down and puts his hand on the armrest of the lawn chair. "Hey, Prudence. How're you today, honey?"

She raises her head to reply, "I am doing okay, Mr. Wolf. And you?" Wolf throws his head back and lets out a loud laugh. Everyone looks his way, then goes back to whatever they were doin'.

"Honey, I have told you time after time to drop the Mr. and just call me Wolf like everyone else does, okay?" Wolf looks to her then back at me. "Prudence, I want to introduce you to one of my closest friends who I consider a like my baby brother. Meet Cadence. I call him C, or kid." She looks directly at me and I'm taken back by her eyes, or by the way she stares intently, like she's able to see my soul and read everything sacred to me.

I step forward with my hand out and immediately Prudence shrinks into the chair, hands reaching to cover her head. Wolf grabs me and pulls me behind him, while he softly speaks to the young woman, "Pru, I would never put you in danger. You know that. He's a good man, young and stupid at times, but deep down where it counts, he's truly a good kid." She lowers her arms trying to shake it off.

Hesitantly she raises a handout in front of her and in a very timid voice says, "Nice to meet you, Cadence."

I lean around Wolf so I can shake her hand gently. "Right back at ya, Prudence. It's nice to meet you, too."

She blushes at my comment and replies, "Please, call me Pru. Everyone here does." Then she awards me with a full smile in my direction and it feel like the sun is high up in the sky shining down on me. She has one of those rare smiles that draws you in holding you there. Like a warm hug. That smile reaches her unusual eyes, which are shining in her face, makin' it all that much more awe-inspiring.

For once in my life this is not a sexual attraction by any means, it's something deeper... it's more, and that shakes me. I've no idea what's happenin' but she stares at me long and hard before she speaks, "Don't be so hard on yourself. You were dealt a rotten hand, but don't let that determine the man you will become. Take care of that little one and all will become clear to you." She rises from the chair and heads toward the little cabin, still holding her Kindle.

Wolf grabs my arm to keep me from fallin' face-first into the lawn chair. "What the fuck, dude? Why're you sharing my Goddamn business with some chick I don't even know? Are you fuckin' her or something?"

Wolf's grasp tightens as he shoves me down. "Watch your mouth, kid. I've not touched Pru in any way, other than to help her. She's been to hell and back. One of my contacts in law enforcement asked me to help her. She was kidnapped and sold into human slavery. I cannot try to image the hell she's been through, and at such a young age. She's here to recover and find what's in her heart so she can figure out what do with her life. I've noticed she has an ability to see *things*, or as we say in the native culture, she has the vision."

I sit here in shock. How did I not know this about

Wolf? "You help total strangers out?" Wolf grabs and pulls me to a picnic bench close and sits on top of it.

Rubbing his hand over his neck, he leans forward and begins to tell me a piece of his story. "C, there's a lot you don't know about me, and one day hopefully I'll share some of it with you. To answer your question, yes. I help others out. It's my way of giving back. Once, a long time ago, someone helped me. They gave me a purpose in life and always had my best interest at heart, no matter what. It wasn't easy because in the beginning I was a fuckin' mess, pushing people away at every available opportunity, but this man never gave up on me. He backed me and stood by me. I owe my life to him and will never forget what he's done for me." Wolf takes a breath, leans back, and continues, "You know whom I speak of, kid. He helped you when you needed it most, too."

My head shoots up out of confusion. "Who, Doc?"

Wolf shakes his head no and replies, "No, kid. It wasn't Doc, it was Des. He not only saved my life, but he gave it purpose, so now I pay it back whenever I can." He points to the cabin that Pru just walked into. "That's just one way I can help. She needs protection, time to heal, and someone who believes in her. The people who had her are looking for her, so she stays here where no one knows her or about this place. She's safe for now."

I look at Wolf with newfound respect. Shit, have I really been so selfish and self-absorbed these last couple of years that I didn't look beyond my own nose to see what's goin' on around me? Lookin' up, I see Wolf watching me, not saying a word. His eyes are intense, but patiently waitin' not sure for what though. I open my mouth then slam it shut cause I can't seem to find the words. "Dude, I'm so fuckin' sorry that my head's been so far up my own ass for so long. You should've told me what you're doin' I would have helped. I may not be as smart and seasoned as you are, but I could pitch in with whatever you need. This is gotta be a lot to take on by yourself."

Wolf lets his breath out, throws his braid over his shoulder so it sits right above his ass. "Thanks, kid, but at the time, you weren't ready to give anything of yourself. Now you're finally finding yourself and are seein' life through clearer eyes. Life is what you make it brother. So, on that note, there's something we need to talk about. Just listen and then give me your thoughts, okay?" I just nod as Wolf continues, "I've already spoken to Trinity, and she agrees. She's even in the process of setting this up for herself. Because you both have had such horrific childhoods and have never truly dealt with them, I think it would be beneficial if both of you saw a therapist. Now, don't get all crazy and defensive, kid. I know that you've talked with one on occasion, but you need to go to one and stick with it, not just when you feel you need it. Both you and Trinity are survivors of sexual abuse at the hands of people who were supposed to protect and take care of you. It's not an easy subject to talk about, but both of you have experienced it. I'm not sure what your plans are with her, but to build a relationship of any kind, you need to be honest and come into the relationship with as little baggage as possible. This shit'll be with both of you forever, kid, but you need to know how to handle it when it pops up. You have a kid comin', and if you two don't have your minds right and your shit together, you'll fuck this child up. You don't want to do that, do you?"

Shaking my head no, I hear him out. "I have contacts that deal with this specific type of abuse and can give you guidance and some building blocks to handle situations when they come up. You'll have to go through exercises to be able to deal with those memories and then put them away. You must remember that they're only memories and they cannot hurt you anymore, unless you keep letting them. It'll make you a stronger man and better father to be able to handle life's situations as they come. If it helps, I have my own shit and I've been seeing a therapist for years. He's helped me develop a technique to not only handle when shit makes it through to the surface, but day-to-day obstacles."

At this news, I'm stunned. Wolf always seems so calm and put together. I don't understand why he would feel the need to see a shrink.

"I want the help, Wolf, I really do. I'm just so fuckin' scared to talk about it. I've never even told the therapist that Doc referred me to the whole truth of what happened. My brand of therapy is all over my skin which I'm also runnin' out of to tattoo and places to pierce." Wolf nods, showing me, he understands exactly what I'm saying. "When the pain is so bad I can't stand it, I get new ink or a piercing. As fucked up as it sounds, the pain from the tat or piercing helps get me over the emotional agony inside."

"I'll give you my guy's information and when you're ready, give him a call. He's cool and doesn't make it seem like you're seeing a shrink just talkin' to a friend, if that's what you're worried about."

"So, explain all of this, bro. How could I not know all of this about you when we spend most of our time together working and hangin' out. I'm a little overwhelmed not to say confused."

Wolf laughs. "Hopefully you see me in a better light than before all of this came out. We all have secrets, or pasts, that we keep close to the vest. What I do here helps me with mine. Didn't mean to keep you out of the loop, but I also didn't think you would even care."

I feel these words deep, because before Trinity I didn't really care about anyone but myself and my needs. I've been one total asshole, that's for sure. "Again, I'm sorry for being such a selfish prick. If there's anything I can contribute or help with, just let me know."

Wolf stands and pulls me to my feet. "Let me give you the grand tour, and then we'll see if you still want to volunteer here. There's a lot going on here, kid, and there are some things I can't show you just yet. You don't have clearance."

"Clearance for what, dude? You got illegal shit going on here with all these people walking around?"

As we walk, Wolf replies, "Not at all, C, but some of what I do is work with different agencies to help survivors move on and start truly living. Let's go around and I'll show you what I mean."

CHAPTER NINETEEN

CADENCE

Stepping out of the shower, I look down at the hard-on I'm sporting. Every time I spend the night at Wolf's with Trinity, I have to come home and whack one off. I'm so fuckin' horny I can't stand it, but since all of this started with finding Trinity, I've made myself a promise to not sleep with anyone until we figure out where she wants to go with us, but it's gettin' harder to do as days turn into weeks. The more time I spend with her, the deeper my feelings for her grow, and that scares the shit out of me. She's such a sweet, funny, and alluring woman. I can't get enough of her sweet nature and amazing sense of humor. She's the girl I met, but now she's so much more since she's able to be herself and not be afraid.

Work is a bitch. I can't believe how busy we have been these last couple of weeks. One of our competitors closed in town, so everyone is bringin' all their auto work to Connelly's, and even though we all thought we had most of our town's repair work, it's now apparent that we didn't, but now we do. Between Archie and me, we are busting out oil changes, tune-ups, and basic repairs, along with all the diagnostic shit I'm responsible for. Thank God Des was able to pull together some funds to get those computerized tools because it has helped me cut time when doin' large repairs on these new computerized cars. n our little town of Tranquility, a lot of folks still have old cars with carburetors and such, which make them easier to work on.

To top it all off, we have the Charity Ride for Fern and Doc, which is only weeks away. Between trying to get donations, getting all the information on the website, getting a hold of all our contacts and such, I have no free fuckin' time. Then there is the weekly, or sometimes twice a week meeting to follow up on everything for the ride. From what Des has told us at the last meeting, he heard back from the lady at the Bone Marrow Foundation, and they have had an influx of donations linked to the charity ride already. So much so, they couldn't be happier and have repeatedly thanked Des for including them. I just hope that with all the donors, they find one for Fern.

I grab a towel with my mind still on Fern. I've noticed that she's starting to look worse. Between the increase in her treatments and the side effects, it's taking a toll on her body and mind. I've tried to help

Doc out as much as I can, but he has taken it upon himself to look out for Trinity and our baby also. He's afraid of her name popping up somewhere, which would make it easier for her father to track her down, if he was looking. He found a doctor who has kept her off their books, but he has still taken an active role in making sure that she and the baby are staying healthy.

Fern has taken Trinity under her wing and has even gone to some of her doctor's appointments with her when she was up to it. I haven't gotten to go because all the appointments are during my workday and the drive to the doctor is thirty to forty minutes away, so I couldn't do it at lunch, but today I'm going to finally hear and see our baby. The excitement and fear have me a mess as I finish brushin' my teeth.

Looking at my reflection in the mirror, I wonder what I was thinking these last couple of years. Between tattoos and piercings, I'm loaded, but now I realize that I've been moving the pain from internally to externally, which now just seems stupid. I have multiple piercings on my face, including my lip, tongue, and eyebrow. I also have both nipples done. For the finale, I have my cock piercings, starting with the Apadravya on the top then all the balls on the underside. I also have the Hafada on my scrotum, but I've had way too many issues with it. I've had more metal on me than most women.

When I go to put the piercing in my dick, changing out the jewelry, I immediately start to harden, just from the touch of my own hand. Fuck, I need to figure this shit out with Trinity because I'm gettin' sick of hand jobs especially by my own hand.

Finishing what I was doing, I reach for the lotion on the counter and pump some into my hand and I begin to rub it up and down the length of my cock. Between the location, piercings, and firm grip, I know I won't last long but I go into my bedroom to finish off. I grab my phone on the way and lie down. Moving my hand in an up and down motion with a slight twist on top, I feel that sweet sensation in my balls. Reaching down, I open up the pictures in my phone to the one of Trinity sleeping. I set it to the side so I can see it, then reach down to grab my balls. This picture has her tits poppin' out of her bra, so I concentrate on that as I begin to thrust faster and squeeze harder until I feel my balls start to tighten. Grabbin' a hold of my cockhead, I pull on my piercing hard, feeling the tingles along my spine shoot to my balls. Releasing the piercing, I run both hands up and down quickly as cum shoots out of the slit in long, creamy ribbons, landing on my stomach and chest.

I continue with the movement as another load shoots out, and then another. Finally, I stop my hand movement and just lie on my bed, trying to catch my breath. Fuck, if a picture of Trinity can bring this response, what's gonna to happen if she ever lets me fuck her again?

As my heart rate slows back to normal, I look over at the clock and realize that I've spent way too much time jackin' off. I've got to get ready to meet both Trinity and Wolf at the doctor's office. I admit, I'm still not too happy with how much time Wolf gets to spend with her, but on the other end of that thought, I'm also glad she's not alone, and more importantly, she's safe.

CHAPTER TWENTY

CADENCE

After fighting traffic for what seemed like forever, I get lost in the medical building, but I finally arrive at the OB/GYN's office. As I enter the room, I hear Trinity's laugh and it hits me in the chest. God, there is just something about her that makes my heart beat a little quicker and my steps a little lighter. I look around, trying to find her and see Wolf first. All the chairs are taken with pregnant women, so he's standin' to the side with his hand lying gently on Trinity's shoulder. I can just make out the conversation when I approach as Wolf is trying to explain that he is not the baby's daddy. Trinity is laughing as he struggles to explain the situation.

As she looks up and notices me, I see a look of complete surprise and happiness. Shit, did she think I wouldn't come? Looking at her, I can't believe she is the same girl we rescued all those months ago. She is actually glowing, and she is absolutely gorgeous. Her rounded belly has popped out and she looks like she is having a baby... my baby. I feel proud that I'm gonna to be a daddy, and she'll be my baby's amazing mother.

Looking at her sittin' there with my child growing in her belly brings tears of happiness to my eyes. Within a month or so, I'm going to be a daddy to some little person who will rely on me for everything, and that shit blows my mind. I'm just now getting the hang of my two kittens at home.

Stoppin' in front of Trinity, I first reach out and grab Wolf's shoulder. "Thanks so much for getting her here. I appreciate it." Wolf just nods, then I lean down in front of Trinity. "How are you doin'? Feeling good today?" I reach out to push her hair behind her ear. To my surprise, she tilts her head into my hand, putting a huge smile on my face. She's been doin' more of this lately; being affectionate, always sitting close to me, rubbing her hand up and down my thigh. I think she's just looking for some form of contact—a connection.

She leans in and tells me that she's doing fine. As we wait for her to be called into the back, Wolf and I begin to talk about the charity ride. A little while later, I hear the door open and a woman's voice calls, "Trinity Vinkers."

As Trinity tries to stand, she can't rock up with her belly throwing her off. She instantly breaks into giggles, which she does a lot of lately for no reason, as both Wolf and I help her up. Wolf let's her go, tellin' her, "I'll meet up with you both at Cadence's later. Good luck."

Both Trinity and I look at him dumbfounded. "Aren't you coming in to see the baby?" I ask.

Wolf's face is one full of shock and awe. "Really? Ya want me there during such an intimate moment?" We both shake our heads yes, so the three of us follow the nurse to a small room.

The nurse doesn't hide whatever it is that she's feeling as she gives us all a disgusted look. "Which one of you is the daddy? Or do you even know?" The sounds that I hear comin' from Wolf and me have the nurse taking a step closer to the door.

Trinity puts a hand on our arms and looks directly into the nurse's eyes and says in her quiet voice, "Bitch, get out of this room and don't come back. Send in your manager because I hope to Christ they don't approve of your ignorance. Get the fuck out of here and be thankful I'm pregnant."

The nurse turns and practically runs out of the room as Trinity starts to shake and her eyes fill with tears. "Oh gosh, what's the matter with me? How could I talk to her like that?"

"Shit, little one. That was awesome. You definitely put her in her place, proud of you." Wolf says excitedly.

I approach her and pull her in for a hug. "Honey, that was fuckin' perfect. I've never seen this side of you, but I like it a lot." I wiggle my eyebrows at her and seein' this makes her laugh.

The door opens and an older woman enters holding a folder. "Miss Vinkers, my nurse tells me that you wanted to see me?"

"Yes. I have a problem with the way your nurse spoke to us and insinuated that because both of these men were with me that I didn't know who the father was. Now regardless of if that were true or not, the apparent ignorance in your employee is uncalled for, especially since I am in my last trimester of pregnancy and don't need any added stress. Per your doctors here." The woman glances at all three of us before settling back on Trinity.

"Well, my name is Mary and I would like to apologize for this unfortunate incident. This isn't the first complaint on this particular nurse, but I can guarantee it will be the last. Please know we value you as a patient and this will not happen again. Give me a few moments and I will be back to do your ultrasound personally, if that's okay?"

Wolf and I nod, but Trinity looks at Mary with wide eyes. "Please don't fire her, Mary. Maybe someone just needs to talk to her, give her some guidance, I guess. I would hate to be responsible for her losing her job."

Mary shakes her head. "Honey, you aren't responsible, she is. Do me a favor? Have a seat up on the table, undo your pants and cover up with the paper blanket provided. Then lift your top, just under your breasts, so that when I come back you are ready to see your baby."

Trinity does as she's told and about ten minutes later, Mary returns. By this time, I'm sweating, pacing, and a nervous wreck. She immediately gets started by taking measurements and checking the baby's heartbeat. Once she writes everything down, she turns out the lights and begins squeezing some sort of goop onto Trinity's belly. She then takes a wand from a machine and starts to roll it over Trinity's belly as Trinity says, "Come meet your baby, Cadence." Then she looks to Wolf. "Come meet your niece or nephew, Uncle Wolf." We are both silenced by her words and come to her side as the machine in front of Mary looks like she's watching something from space.

As she moves the wand in circles around Trinity's belly, I could swear that I see a foot—no wait—is that a hand with fingers? I can feel my body tremble as Mary focuses the screen and voilà! There is a complete baby with a head, arms, legs, feet, and hands. You can even see the baby sucking its thumb, which is so fuckin' cute that it makes my heart skip a beat. This is my flesh and blood... *MY* kid. Holy shit Motherfucker.

I look over to Wolf and see him staring at the screen with such awe and wonder on his face. Do I look like him right now? "Are you sure that you don't want to know what you're having? I've got a clear shot if you do."

Both Trinity and I look at each other and say together, "NO!"

Mary snaps some photos for us, and even one for Uncle Wolf.

Once the appointment is over, Wolf takes off, telling us that he'll see us for dinner. We head in separate directions, Trinity riding back with me. We make our way toward my truck when Trinity stops suddenly and grabs my arm. I look at her and follow her eyes that are staring at a man with nothing but contempt on his face. The old guy starts to walk in our direction as I grab Trinity and place her behind me. As he gets closer to us, he starts yellin' like a crazy man, "You little bitch! I wondered where you ran off. Who the fuck's the freak with all the tattoos and shit on his face?" He looks down at Trinity's belly then says to me, "Look here, you goddamn freak. I want to talk to my daughter, so you best move your ass aside before I do it for you."

I just glare at him and don't even bother to say a word, but he's not finished. "I should have beat you both to death, you and your bastard..." Before he gets the rest of his sentence out, my arm is already wound up, heading straight for his face. The sound of my fist hittin' flesh and cartilage makes me half ass try to rein in my anger for his blood.

The old guy's nose is definitely broken, and his lip is split. I look down at the fucker and tell him, "That's for how I found her in that shitty trailer you live in. In fact, you deserve a couple more for all the bruises and broken ribs you gave her. Just for the record, you no good son of a bitch, that baby is mine and I could kill you right now with my bare hands for threatenin' the safety of it and its mother, do you understand me? You better stay the fuck away or I'll take her myself to press charges against you and your loser friends. I know everything. Forget that you ever knew her and never come lookin' for her again, or you will deal with me."

As her father looks up, he visibly pales at what he's looking at, and then I hear, "And that goes for me to, you motherfucker. Stay away from her or I will personally remove your sorry ass from this earth, and believe me, no one will miss you or care." I turn to see Trinity in Wolf's arms, holding her tightly. I don't know why, but the smile she gives me, like she's proud of me, makes me turn back to her father while swingin' my fist, hitting him square in the side of his face.

"What the fuck was that for?' he asks.

I move to Trinity's other side, "Just a parting reminder to stay the FUCK away, old man." He's shaken, but he still glares at his daughter with such hatred that I begin to worry for her.

Roman Vinkers points his finger at Trinity and rages, "Bitch, you better watch your back because when you least expect it, I will be there. You're mine, you stupid little whore, and as far as your little bastard baby? You ain't delivered it yet..." That's it. I don't even recognize the sound that comes out of me as I lunge at Roman like a wild animal. We both tumble to the ground as I pound my fist repeatedly into his face. I barely register the screaming comin' from behind me because I am so intent on killing this asshole who just threatened not only his own daughter, but also my child.

I feel strong hands pulling me off Roman and I

watch as others help the old fuck to his feet. There is a crowd around us now, including one of the town deputies. As I struggle for air, I hear him ask, "What the hell is going on here?" People in the crowd start shouting out their interpretations of what went down, then the deputy looks at Wolf. "Can you tell me what exactly happened, big man?"

Wolf scowls at him but manages to keep his calm while relaying what happened. "That man, Roman Vinkers, verbally attacked his daughter with threats of violence and death against her and her unborn child. That is when Cadence stepped in to show him the error of his words."

The crowd immediately quiets down to hear what the deputy is going to say. The deputy looks over at Trinity, who is now clinging to me and asks her, "Miss, is what Wolf said correct? Did he threaten you?"

Shaking her head and wiping the tears from her face, she responds, "He said that he should have beat me and my baby to death, and to watch my back, insinuating that he is coming for me and will hurt my child when I least expect it." Taking a deep breath she looks directly into the deputy's eyes and asks, "How long do you have to press charges when someone abuses you, physically and sexually? To be clear, I am talking about sexual assault against me, his daughter since I was the age of thirteen."

Her father lunges for her but is stopped by Wolf, who reaches over and grabs his shoulder, spinnin' him around, and punchin' him in the jaw, cracking it instantly. The deputy reaches behind him for his cuffs and goes through the steps to arrest Trinity's father. As the crowd breaks up, Trinity suddenly grabs her stomach and screams, "Something is wrong! My stomach oh my God it hurts really bad." Then she goes limp and passes the fuck out, in my arms.

CHAPTER TWENTY-ONE

TRINITY

I'm lounging on Cadence's couch in his apartment, watching him in the kitchen as I play with his kittens. They are lying on either side of me, purring as I run my hands along their little bodies. Boots and Kibble are both so cute that I can't get enough of them.

I try to relax, but the day's events are running through my mind. I think about what the doctor told me after the incident with my dad. She explained that my blood pressure was elevated due to stress, which caused stress to the baby and my body, so she prescribed rest. That's why I'm watching Cadence make dinner. The deputy waited to let us know that my father was arrested for publicly threatening physical violence against his pregnant daughter, which was confirmed by witness statements taken at the scene. No charges would be brought against Cadence or Wolf for protecting me, as my father came at me first. Roman would be in jail until he was seen by a judge and given a bail amount. If I wanted to file charges against him for sexual and physical abuse, I would have to go to the station and file a report for him to be arrested, which I did once I left the doctor's office, but there was a very high possibility that he would still get out on bail until a case was set against him.

Cadence comes around the counter to sit next to me while lifting my legs up and putting them across his lap. He starts to rub my feet and my eyes start to close as the tensions of the day start to leave my body. "So tell me about the Charity Ride for Fern. I know it's pretty soon, right?"

"It's in three weeks, so I'm gonna be busy tryin' to get everything together. We still have a lot to do and the MCs are gonna start rolling in soon, so Des is making sure that we are all prepared." Putting his hands on my upper thighs, he continues to rub the tension in my body away. "This has to work, Trinity. Fern is getting worse by the day. Every time I go over to their house she looks thinner and weaker, and she's startin' to lose her faith and will to fight." As he speaks, I can hear the emotion behind his words. "If the charity ride brings donors for the Bone Marrow Foundation, the chance to find a donor for Fern is so much greater, not to mention the money we are raisin' to help both Fern and Doc with their ridiculous outrageous bills."

I grab his hands in mine and hold them tight. "I'm here for you, Cadence. I love both Fern and Doc, so whatever you need, know that I will help in any way I can."

He holds on to my hands and pulls me into a sitting position, which isn't easy being a little over eight months pregnant. I let out a grunt and before I can stop it, an extremely long, loud fart sneaks out and man does it stink. My face instantly turns red as I try to free my hands to cover my face. I try to take a breath and snort in air, causing a coughing fit. I wipe my face of the spit that dribbles out of my mouth while my body tenses as I feel some leakage, which are drips of urine leaking out into my panties. "Holy Christ! I can't believe this is happening to me. All of this because you tried to sit me up. I am so fucking embarrassed, so don't even look at me right now... Please don't look." I raise my head to glance his way, only to see his body shaking from laughing so hard at me.

Once he finally inhales, he again lets out a roar of laughter so loud and hard that he has to hold his sides. "Shit, girl, you crack me the fuck up. Don't ever change, baby. According to that pregnancy book, this is all normal shit so don't get too worked up, but to go from reading about it to actually hearin' and seein' it firsthand, it's the highlight of my Goddamn year." I feel a moment of wanting to run from this embarrassing situation, but out of everything he just said, I really only heard that he read the book. He read the pregnancy book. I haven't even read the whole book, just parts of it. What does it mean that he read the book?

Never being in a relationship with a man, I'm mortified at what just happened, and it didn't help that he was sitting right next to me, laughing his ass off. Before I know it, I'm angry, so I reach over and slap the back of his head open-handed, "What the hell is so frigging funny, huh?" He tries to stop laughing but again grabs his sides. As I watch him bust a gut over my shameful behavior, I realize that I have never seen him look so relaxed and carefree. I start to lose my anger and feel my own laughter rising up to explode. We both sit here and laugh hysterically for what seems like forever. And every once in a while we would here a toot and start cracking up all over again.

This is what Wolf walks in on, carrying some bags and flowers with him. "What's so funny, you two? Let me in on the joke."

I reach for Cadence's hand, still laughing and shaking my head. "Please don't tell him."

"We're all family, babe. Don't be embarrassed because we always share our shit. Get used to it. You're one of us now."

Suddenly filled with such emotion, I stop laughing completely and begin to sob uncontrollably. After a couple of minutes go by, Wolf leans over touching my shoulder. "Little one, are you okay? What is the matter? You can tell us what's wrong."

I wipe my nose on my sleeve. Looking up at him with tears still falling down my cheeks and eyes swollen from crying, I tell him bluntly, "I farted."

Wolf looks from me to Cadence. "Hormones, dude. They are a bitch from what I hear." This breaks the uncomfortable moment as we all begin to laugh again.

Later we are all sitting at the dining room table eating, drinking, and just enjoying each other's company when Cadence gets up and goes to one of the bedrooms and calls out, "Be right back." Both Wolf and I look confused but continue to eat our dinner; barbecue chicken with baked potatoes, rolled in cracked sea salt, along with a medley of fresh vegetables steamed with some olive oil. The best part for me was that I could see dessert sitting on the counter. Looking at Wolf, I ask, "Did you know that he could cook like this? I'm totally blown away and shocked."

Wolf shakes his head. "I've only been here a couple of times, and we usually hang outside with the kittens, having beers."

As we linger over our meal, Cadence returns to the table with a large package in his hands and puts it down by Wolf and sits. Glancing at the box, he asks, "What's this, kid? What have you gone and done now?"

Shaking his head as he stuffs some chicken into his mouth, Cadence won't look Wolf in the eyes, but he says, "It's something from me to you for all you have done over the last couple of months for Trinity, our baby, and me. I can't thank you enough and I don't want you to think that we take it, or you, for granted, so just open the fuckin' box already. It's not a big deal asswipe."

Wolf moves his plate to the side, "C, this dinner would have been enough. With the baby coming, you don't need to be spending your money on anything but your family and the future. I know your intentions and that you mean well, so thanks, kid. We're family, and this is what family does."

Pulling the heavy box in front of him, he tries to open the top but grabs for the huge knife on the table, cutting the tape off the top. He rips the two halves open, looks inside, then looks up at Cadence with shock apparent on his face, "How the fuck did you get this? It was sold when I went back." Cadence grins back at him as I sit in the dark. Wolf reaches in to remove the packing and with both hands, he pulls out a huge statue of wolves. It looks to be a pack of them and they're all colors and sizes, including some pups. It's mounted on a highly polished piece of oak so you can display it on a table. The detail of the piece amazes me. I glance at Cadence, who's watching Wolf carefully, and that's when I notice it. On the back of the piece is a plate with writing.

As Wolf reads the poem about brothers, the emotions that pour out of his voice are overwhelming. At one point he closes his eyes to take a deep breath. His body is slightly trembling as he continues to read the metal plate. I can't stand the suspense, so I get up and walk over to Wolf. He puts a hand up to hold me off for a moment, and then he raises his eyes to Cadence.

Never in my entire life have I seen such open and loving emotion in a man's eyes for another man. Not at all in a sexual way, but a bond in friendship and family that can overwhelm you but also make you feel whole. Wolf places the statue down so I can read the wording as he walks to Cadence. He grabs him by the shoulders, pulling him in close. "Totally feel the same, C. Our friendship has become one of the most important things to me. I consider you my little brother, and I will treasure this gift until my last day on this earth. These last couple of months you have done so well with therapy, Trinity, and the baby. I couldn't be prouder of you guys. I am honored to be part of this," as he motions with his hands, "whatever it may become."

"Oh my gosh. That is so... I don't know, but Cadence? That poem is frigging awesome." At my loss of words, both men drop their arms and snicker at me as they clear the table.

CHAPTER TWENTY-TWO

TRINITY

I watched as Wolf and Cadence carried the statue down to the big guy's truck, knowing he didn't need help, but they needed some time alone. They talked for a bit and then he left. We all spent the rest of the evening talking, playing cards, and taking it easy. The kittens are already cuddled together on the bed as I get ready to hit the hay myself. I've been holding Cadence off from having sex since they rescued me all those months ago. I've gradually started letting my guard down by having make-out sessions with no sex. He gets me off and I get him off, but that's all I've given him. This has all happened slowly over the last five months, and I want to give him the same thing I want. He's been here for me, staying with me every night and working all day long, so I know his spare time is always spent with me.

I can hear him closing everything up and turning off the stereo, along with the lights. I've made my decision and I pray that this time, I don't won't live to regret it.

I go to the bathroom, take off my clothes, and turn on the shower. Pulling my hair up into a clip, I step under the water to rinse off this day. I want to wash off all the terrible words and the disgusting people that I've had to deal with. I want my mind clear before I go back into that room to be with Cadence.

Since stopping to buy a few things to stay here tonight, I bought a razor because, really, I can't imagine what it looks like down there, probably a woman forest. Not to mention my hormones are completely out of my control, so I feel self-conscious about the act of having sex without doing any ha know. Grooming. I take my time and shave everything I can to the best of my very pregnant belly and hope I don't look like I got a bad haircut down there. Rinsing off, I step out, wrapping up in a towel. I start to put on lotion because it's one of the things that I found as a luxury once I got out of that hellhole. It's stupid, but it's something that makes me feel nice. Once I finish, I brush my teeth and dry my hair with the towel.

As I enter the room, he's already in bed, lying on his side under the covers, playing with the kittens as they try to sleep. He glances up as I walk toward the bed, and he looks completely shocked. "Babe, you okay? Do you need one of my T-shirts to sleep in?" I continue to move closer to the bed and when I'm within reach, I drop the towel and slowly enter the bed.

I decide that I'm going to get straight to the point. I

move close and go straight for his nipple piercing. I rub on it, and then I tug it, getting a sexy groan from him. I look down and see that his erection is already forcing his briefs out, and I can see the head of his cock.

Looking into his eyes, I see his desire and it's all for me. "I want you, Cadence, and not just to play. I want to feel you inside of me again so bad, so please touch me, taste me, make love to me."

Wasting no time, he pulls me to him as his hands grab my ass cheeks, but neither one of us give any thought to my extended belly getting in the way.

"Oh my God, Cadence. I'm disgusting to you, aren't I? I wasn't even thinking about how I look to you. I just wanted to put everything behind us and move forward, but I can't be attractive to you or even be able to please to you to right now."

He doesn't say a word, but he looks me straight in the eyes as he places his hand to cup my face, then he begins to move down to my breast and squeezes a handful, causing me to push into his hand. "Do you know that I jack off to your picture? Do you know that seeing your body filled out the way it is, is such a turn-on for me because it's you? It's your face and your body that gets me off, nothing and no one else. No other woman measures up to you, baby, whether you're heavy with my child or not, but you've got curves that you didn't have before, and they make me mad with lust for you. You've gotta see that. There has been no one else, Trinity, and I don't want there to be. I want you and only you. I can't change the past, but I will work every day to be the man you want in your life, in your bed, and the father to your baby. We just need to give this a go and instead of saying let's give it a try, let's say this is it. I want you and I know you want me. This is it for me, Trinity, and all I want is you. Please, baby. Just let me in."

I give him a nod and he starts to play with my nipples again, but I want more, so I take his hand and move it to my core. I start to move his hand around where I need it even though I'm sure my face is blushing a bright pink. He keeps eye contact with me, and I find that I like him watching me as I enjoy this.

After releasing the air in his lungs, he stops to roll me onto my side with my back to his front. He leans forward and moves my hair aside to place small kisses along my neck. Then, he starts to move down my back, adding kisses all the way down my spine as he slowly moves down my body. He sits up and uses his hands to separate my legs from behind, causing me to roll over a little more so that he can have better access. Not knowing what to do with my hands, I pull a pillow down to have an anchor.

With my backside spread open to him, he grabs my ass and gives it a squeeze. I squeal from the pressure because he's squeezing so hard, but then he begins to massage both of my ass cheeks while pushing and pulling them out. I feel his thumbs move to just around my asshole and he begins to apply pressure to that area. As he continues, his intensity grows, and I feel the tip of one of his thumbs press onto my puckered hole a few times, but he doesn't force it in, he just applies enough pressure to have me almost grinding my ass into his thumb. He moves his other hand, separating my slick labia and tapping his finger on my clit.

"Oh my God! Please don't stop. Keep going." He chuckles as I feel him thrust two fingers inside of me, pushing in deep and retreating to push harder into me. He begins to thrust faster, adding one more finger inside of me while still keeping pressure on my ass. I begin moving my hips and I feel myself clenching tighter, but then he stops and all I can do is whimper. He moves back and pulls me so that I'm now on my back.

"You're fuckin' breathtaking, Trinity. I could look at you forever. Pregnancy definitely agrees with you." I smile at him, and he places my hands above my head. "Leave them here, okay? Hang on to the headboard, but don't let them come down. Trust me, I wouldn't do anything to hurt you. I promise."

I nod as the anticipation increases and I place my fingers around the wooden rungs in the headboard. Cadence starts at my shoulders and moves his hands down to start pinching and caressing my breasts. He takes my nipple in between his fingers and lightly pulls. I moan deep in my throat as he leans over one and bites down softly. He continues to nibble and then bite down, then going over it with his tongue to soften the bite. Finally, he just closes his lips around my taut nipple and sucks hard. The pressure I feel is a heat that runs down my entire body, all the way directly to my core. I have to clench my legs together to try and relieve the pressure, but that makes it worse. I need something more.

Cadence moves all the way down to where I need him the most and there it is. His pierced tongue presses flatly onto my clit and I scream as I feel something more than pressure start in my lower belly. He continues, but then he starts to lick in slow, lazy movements with his pierced tongue. I feel like I'm going to come apart. "Cadence, you can't stop. You have to make this pressure go away. You have to fuck me, you have to."

I'm down to begging and pleading. He keeps licking as he adds his fingers and keeps a rhythm of thrusting in and out of me while sucking on my clit. "That's it, Cadence, I'm so close..." And I explode. He keeps at it as one orgasm turns immediately into two. I feel him licking the cum that's coming out of me greedily. Gasping for air, I thrash my head from side to side, slowly coming down from the most intense sexual moment of my life.

Cadence sits up and I watch him as he removes his fingers and brings them to his lips, sticking each finger into his mouth one by one. "Baby, you taste like Heaven. So fuckin' good," he says with a wicked smile. I move my head to the side, embarrassed at his over-the-top action and comment. He moves up to lie down to face me. I can see my desire smeared all over his face.

"Baby, I want you to taste yourself on my lips. I want you to know what I mean when I say how good it is." He lowers his face to mine until his lips touch mine. I open for him, allowing him to deepen the kiss as our tongues dance. I reach down to play with his cock just as the baby kicks really hard. "Holy shit!"

I roll my body into a fetal position and take deep breaths. "What's the matter? Fuck, did I hurt you?"

Raising my eyes, he sees the laughter in them. "No. It's just the baby making itself known. Probably wants to join our party. Give me your hand and feel this." He reaches out as I grab his hand and press it hard to the side of my belly. Immediately his eyes widen. He's feeling something like a little hand or foot pushing his hand out and away. I watch his expressions of absolute shock and joy as it happens again and again. We lie here with our hands on my belly, letting our baby have precious time with us.

After what feels like forever after the baby stops, I look at him. "So, are we going to finish what you started?" As I reach down and begin stroking his cock, his mind shifts from fatherhood to sex in two point five seconds.

Getting off the bed, he kneels at the edge and gently pulls me down to him. Raising my hips entirely off the bed, he lets them fall on his upper thighs, "Baby, are you sure it's safe with you being so far along? I don't think I can be all gentle and shit."

I laugh and tell him, "Cadence, couples have sex up until the day the baby is born, now quit talking and get busy."

He looks excited as he reaches to the side of the bed

where he grabs a condom from the drawer of the nightstand. He rips it open and starts to put it on but then he comes to a complete stop. He pulls the condom off as I watch with wide eyes. "What's the matter? Why are you stopping?"

He clears his throat as his hand goes up and down his length. "Baby, if we're gonna do this, I want to do it right this time. I want to make it special. I want you to have a night where it's all about you, something you've never had. Let's just mess around tonight and give me tomorrow to show you how wonderful you are before I completely rock your world."

"I have to admit I'm a little disappointed, but if it's important enough for you to stop, then I'm willing to wait for you to do whatever you feel you need to do first. But until then, can you do that thing you just did at the same time I get you off?"

That's right. Hormonal and I have no shame.

~Cadence~

All day I've been running all over town to get what I need. I've been going off a list of things that I was told to get by Fern, Dee, Willow, and even Archie. Looking in my car, I realize I didn't have a clue, and I'm thankful to the ladies for their direction.

Arriving home, I'm glad that Trinity isn't here as

time is needed to get my place ready for my big night with her. The kittens both come running out, wanting to play so I take a couple of minutes to scratch both of their bellies and throw the ball with the bell in it. After I exhaust them, I give them their treats and start to get everything in order. First, the sparkling juice goes in the fridge. Next I arrange the cut-up fruit with the whole strawberries on a plate with the bowl in the middle for whipped cream, just like Dee Dee told me to. Then I look around and realize that my place needs some straightening up. The last couple of months since Trinity came back into my life, I've spent my time at the garage, Wolf's ranch, or here. Not taking time to clean regularly like I used to, the place looks a wreck.

Once I take about an hour to get that situated, I start pulling out the candles, placing them around the rooms. Trinity has never been treated special but in all my years, I've never done this for a woman. So, this is a first for both of us.

Next, I work in the bathroom, putting flowers out like Fern suggested on the counter in the pretty little vase I bought. Then I add pillar candles around the huge, jetted tub I have, partially filling it, and put the rose petals gently in the water. Remembering what Fern said, I lightly place on top of the water and don't fill it too much because when we go in, I will have to warm the water up, so I have to leave room to run hot water.

I place the remaining candles around the room, lighting them and closing the window. Finally, putting the remaining petals on the bed, I step back and look at my work. I'm impressed and shocked at myself to be going through so much to get a piece of ass. Shit, that's not at all what she is, and I know it. She's becoming my heart and soul more and more every day. Not to mention the mother of my unborn baby. Hearin' the doorbell, I wonder who the fuck is here.

Going to the door, I look through the glass before opening it. "Couldn't leave it alone, could ya? You had to come and see."

Wolf laughs as he enters. "Dude, you should be doing those romantic '*how to*' shows on TV. This looks great. Trinity will be pleasantly surprised, so nice job, kid."

I can't help it; I glow with Wolf's approval. "So, what's up? Is this the only reason you're here? Do you want a beer or something?"

Wolf nods then heads to the middle island, sitting on a stool. "A couple of things, actually. First, I didn't think you would go this far, so I had Pru pick this up for your big night."

I look at the fancy bag. "What is it?"

Shaking his head, he replies back, "Shit, don't know and don't want to know. It is a special nightie or something. When I was telling Pru what you had planned, she immediately demanded I take her to that store so she could pick something up for Trinity. You know how women can get, so I did what I was told."

Laughing together, I go to the bedroom and place the bag on the corner of the bed, then head back to where Wolf still sits. "Okay, just tell me. I know there is something on your mind."

"When we were at the store, Pru got really quiet and almost spooked when she was looking out the window. It turns out that Roman, along with another man who was coming out of a diner with him, were the fucking assholes who abducted her and sold her to that freak Axe had to rescue her from. She had no problem identifying them, but she could only identify one by name, and that was Roman Vickers. After talking to Axe though, it isn't enough to arrest them because it is her word against theirs. I want to encourage you to be watchful. I don't believe that Roman is going away. He'll be a problem until we make him not one, so we have to keep our guards up. He's a very dangerous man; I see this now."

After spending a couple of minutes discussing Roman with Wolf, I promise to stay on guard for both Trinity and me, and he will watch out for us too. As he stands to go, he puts a hand on my shoulder and looks me in the eyes. "After seeing how far you went to make Trinity feel special and loved, I'm really proud of you, kid. Not just for this, but for steppin' up and being there for her. You didn't need to *"be with her"* to help her, but I think you see Trinity for the rare gem she truly is. I wish the two of you all the best and if you need anything, you know that I am always here. As sappy as this sounds, especially coming from me, I can't wait to see my little niece or nephew."

"That means more to me than you will ever know,

brother. I hate to even say this to you because your head is going to get bigger than it already is, but since I came on board here, you've always been my idol, so your words will always mean a ton to me. Thanks, man."

"Funny you say that. You've always been my idol, kid. The shit you went through didn't break you, but it did make you stronger, and when the right woman came into your life, you got your head out of your ass and went after what you wanted; what you needed. That is something to look up to. See ya later. Give the little one my love."

After Wolf's departure, I try to clear my mind of his news, deciding that it has to be thought on, but not tonight. I go about preparing everything for our special dinner. The steaks are marinating, potatoes are in the oven, lightly dusted with a mix of sea salt, pepper, along with butter, and my special rub, and the vegetables steaming on the stovetop. I go into the spare bath to shower and shave. Goin' into my bedroom, I pick up the bag from Fern. Fuck, I can't believe that I'm gonna wear this shit, but for Fern and Trinity, I'll do just about anything. Fuck with the ride only weeks away, people are getting things ready. Even people are showin' up early to lend a hand. This place will be bursting at the seams. I say a quick prayer that we find a match; there is no other solution.

Pullin' out the nice beige cargo slacks, I rip the tags off and pull them on. I'm going commando tonight. Then grabbing the shirt, a nice, casual button-up shirt, I throw it on as well. Walking toward the bathroom, I run my hands through my hair. I quickly brush my teeth, spray on the cologne from Fern, and I'm ready. Looking up into the mirror, I'm a little taken aback. Damn, I look good. Movin' to look from side to side and then over my shoulder, I'm so involved with my look that I don't hear anything until Des's voice booms through the apartment, "Look, Dee. He now thinks he a fuckin' model for Christ's sake."

I jump, as they scared me shitless for a minute. After the talk with Wolf, who wouldn't be. "Fuck, Des. Have you ever heard of knockin'?" Both Des and Dee break out into laughter. Dee snorts and bends over as she laughs, holding her sides. I look at them for a minute then join in with a huge howl of my own laughter. The pressure instantly leaves my body. They're just what the doctor ordered. "What brings you two here?"

"Just checking to make sure you're okay, Cadence," Dee Dee says as she walks toward me, putting her hands on my cheeks. "Great job, kiddo. I'm very impressed with the effort you took. She's a lucky lady to have you in her corner. Never forget that as blessed as you are to have her, she is also as blessed to have you. You are a first-class choice for her. Love you, Cadence. Always have, always will. You are a such wonderful man with such a bright future, and we can't wait to meet the baby. Hope you know we plan to spoil that little baby, and you can't stop us. Fern and I have already made plans." She kisses my cheek and walks toward Des. "Baby, I'll be in the truck."

Des nods then catches my eye. We stare at each other and finally Des gives me a chin lift. "One of the best and worst days of my life was when I found you. It was bad because of the shape you were in, but it was the best because I found a kid who would find a place in my heart, one I couldn't love more if he was my own. You've done a great job with the upgrades to the apartment, by the way. It just goes to show how hard you've worked to become a better man, makin' a home for yourself, and settin' down roots. If you keep it up, I see a long and happy future for both of ya." Handin' over a little bag, he says, "Just as you requested, here it is. Good luck, kid." Walking to my side, he pulls me in for a hug and then pats my back before he turns and walks out.

I stumble to the couch and sit down. I kinda of knew everyone cared for me but I never actually realized how much I cared for them in return.

After getting myself together, I finish the chores while I wait. As I hear her giggling with Willow and Archie, I stand at the kitchen island with a bouquet of exotic flowers in my hand. When the door opens, first comes in Willow, followed by Archie. I wait patiently until Trinity finally walks in and I watch as her body comes to an immediate stop. Willow grabs her bags and purse from her, as Archie guides her toward me with a smile. "As requested. Here she is, Cadence. Oh, and by the way, the place looks awesome." She turns to Trinity and softly says to her, "One day I hope to find a guy who's willing to do all of this romance shit for me." She finishes with a small laugh, but I see the sadness in her eyes.

I lean over to Archie, pullin' her to me and whispering in her ear, "Baby, he's out there but remember, he'll have to get through all of us. We have to make sure he's good enough for you, Precious." Kissing her forehead, I glance down to see the surprise on her face before she once again puts on her badass lookin' face.

"Whatever," she says as she turns and heads to the door. "Have fun."

Willow comes around and gives both of us a hug and tells me, "Knew you had it in you. Love you, Cadence."

As I watch them both walk out, I turn to Trinity. "So, are you ready for your night?" She just nods, still in shock.

Getting her comfortable on the couch and playing with the kittens, I check to make sure that everything is okay. I put on the stereo and the song "All of Me" by John Legend fills the room. Lookin' back at her, I see the look of utter surprise on her flushed face. Runnin' my hand down her cheek, I lean in and say, "This song says it all, Trinity. Listen closely to every word."

I leave her to start the grill up and put on the steaks. With everything goin' as planned, I go back into the house.

I get this empty feeling in the pit of his stomach as

my hands start to shake. Sweating like crazy, I wipe my face down with a paper towel, then I go to grab the sparking juice and tray of fruit to take out for us to snack on. I'm so fuckin' nervous that I stumble and almost drop the tray in her lap. She sits up and helps me place it on the coffee table so I'm able to sit and relax for a minute. Christ, is this what happens when you fall in love with someone? With that question, I immediately start to calm down when I realize what is going on internally. My body is finally catching up with my heart.

"What's all of this, Cadence? I'm so confused, but not in a bad way. I feel like I just walked into a romance novel by one of my favorite authors, Kristen Ashley or one of my other favorites like Madeline Sheehan, Jaci J, Chelle Bliss, or even Nina Levine who are a little bit rougher. But you're not a biker, badass, or an Alpha. Don't get me wrong, you could be, but I see you more of like a Tate, Max, or even maybe a Mitch. They are all some of my favorites." She giggles and I can't help but laugh too. I have no fuckin' idea what she's jabbering about, but I love listening to anything she has to say.

"Honey, I'm better than any guy in your books because I'm real standing right in front of you, and I'll be here for you to the end of my days. To answer your question, all of this is my way of trying to make up for letting you down and trying to show you what you truly mean to me."

Trinity looks at me with a blinding smile on her face as she says, "You know that when we first became friends, it was your personality, humor, and just plain goofiness that pulled me toward you like a magnet, right? I never imagined we would have been anything more, and really, we never were, but as much as I never wanted to admit it, I loved you, Cadence Powers. Through all the good and bad that we've been through, I still love you."

She leans in and places a very soft, passionate kiss on my lips. As she goes to pull away, I grab her and bring her back. With my lips almost touching hers, I look directly into her eyes. "Trinity Vinkers, I love you, too. I love your face, your body, your heart, and for carrying our baby with reverence and love. I feel you in my soul, Trinity. You really are my other half—my better half—and you make me want to be a better man. I want to be a man you can be proud of and never feel you have to question or doubt. I'll always be here for you, and you'll never have to worry about anything ever again."

I give her a soft, lingering kiss. "Dinner will be ready in a bit, and you need to eat, not only for you, but for the '*little Tiny*.' It's gonna know what a good cook Daddy is." I place my hand on her belly and feel a small flutter, followed by a strong push. "Shit, our kid is gonna be strong."

We relax into each other, snacking on the fruits and talk and share about our day.

~Trinity~

. . .

After a spectacular dinner, I stand to clean up as Cadence says, "Baby, leave it. I got this, so just relax." I love this sweet side of him, but right now this pregnancy and last night have me so horny that it's all I can think about.

Cadence grabs my hand and walks me down the hall into the master bedroom that is softly lit by all the candles around the room. Everything about tonight feels magical.

"Not too predictable, is it, baby?" I just shake my head while being directed to the master bathroom. Cadence leans down to turn on the water. "I'm going to clean up and I want you to take a relaxing bath. Dee told me about oils that help you to relax, so I got you a few and they are sittin' right there. When you're done, put on what's in the bag that's sitting on the bed and wait for me, okay?"

"Sure," is all I get out before he leaves me to it.

~Cadence~

Drying my hands off on the towel, I head down to the master bedroom. When I enter, I'm blown away at seeing her in my bed with her long, blonde hair fanned out over her shoulders. I obviously took too long, and now she's curled up, sleeping.

She's wearin' the nightie from the bag, and it fits her perfectly. It's not one of those trashy looking ones, it's sexy and classy, like it's meant to be worn by her perfection. I feel my cock harden just by looking at her in it.

I walk to the bed, removing my clothes as I go. I grab a few condoms, place them on the nightstand, and crawl into bed behind her. I start to caress her shoulders, running my fingers down her back and squeezing her cheeks, pushing my hardness against her back and her body tenses for a minute before pushing back against my cock with a small moan. Reaching around, I find her nipple and begin pinching it lightly while she grinds farther back into me. I move from her breast, trailin' my hand down over her bump to her center and find that she didn't bother with panties. That right there is sexy as shit. Once I slip a finger against her clit I can feel how wet she already is. "Oh fuck, baby. I love feeling how fuckin' wet you are for me."

Running circles on her swollen bundle of nerves, I pull her closer and raise the satin material, so my cock rests between her legs. I get my fingers nice and wet then push them into her, looking for that sweet spot deep inside her pussy. It's hidden up high, but with a little time, I find it and start rubbing that piece of skin with my finger and continue to concentrate on that spot.

Her body is thrusting onto my fingers when suddenly I want to taste her, so I move to place her on her back and situate myself between her spread legs. I lick and suck as her juices fill my mouth, wanting to get her off in every way I can. I have my girl moaning and bucking her hips up for me as she comes for me again and again. I love the sound of her screaming out my name every time she orgasms, telling me she can't take it anymore, but her body tells me something else, so I keep givin' it to her.

I finally decide that we've both had enough. It's time to give ourselves what we both really want, so I reach over and grab a condom. I can feel as Trinity watches me put it on, being careful not to snag it on my piercings. "Little late for those, don't you think? Hello, already pregnant here."

I let out a laugh. "Baby, until I get tested, I don't want to take any chances, but I think I'll go get that shit done real soon."

I take my cock and push it through her wetness, then tap her clit with the head of my rock-hard cock. I do this repeatedly, just because I like to watch her facial expressions with each feeling she gets. I laugh again when she tells me to get inside of her, so I do as I'm told. I slowly begin to enter her tight, wet pussy. I feel her walls clamp down each time I pull out and push back in. Fuck, she's tight. "Please, Cadence. I don't want slow and sweet, so stop fucking around and fuck me."

I'm only shocked by her words for a second, but then I grab her hips and watch as I push all the way in until my balls touch her ass. "You feel so fuckin' good—tight and wet..." I lose control as my hips take on a mind of their own and start to move, slowly at first but then I'm fucking her like it's my first fuckin' time. No control. Watching her beautiful, full tits bounce each time I thrust in makes me lose my mind just a little bit more. I'm so consumed with her that I lose my rhythm time and time again. Holdin' her legs up, I watch as my cock disappears into her pussy to come out each time wetter than before. The pressure is overwhelming as my balls start to tighten up, telling me that I'm close. "Trinity, come for me, baby. I want to watch as you orgasm with my cock inside of you."

"Rub my clit, Cadence. I'm so close," she says, so I start rubbin' her clit with just enough pressure to have her arch her back. Between my cock and fingers, I finally get to watch this beautiful woman lose complete control, and it's fucking perfection. She's meeting each thrust with one of her own and I can feel the walls of her pussy startin' to clench down. Once I feel her tense up, I know the time has come so I take my fingers and press down harder on her clit, while pumping into her with a vengeance.

Her entire body goes still for a moment, then she suddenly screams, "Oh God! Oh God, don't stop. Please don't stop! I'm about to come..." Her pussy tightens even more, and the pressure feels so good that I finally shoot my load into the condom. I continue to pump into her because I have never had an orgasm as hard, intense, and long as this one.

I finally start to slow down, and when I look at her, she has the most satisfied and blissful look in her eyes. We stare at each other for a few moments, just takin' each other in, and then I say, "Let me take care of this. I'll be right back."

I go to the bathroom to clean myself up and once I'm done, I get a warm washcloth and go back out to clean Trinity up. While I'm doing this, I watch as she yawns and slowly starts to fade off. I've put down the washcloth and I rub her legs, helping her to relax and drift off. Once I know she's out, I cover her up and walk out to the couch, where immediately Kibble and Boots are at my side, looking for some attention.

As I pet both of my growing kittens, I feel such a sense of calm. For the first time in my life, I feel complete. Lookin' around my place, I see just some of the things that I've accomplished, then I reach for the box that Des gave me from the coffee table. I feel no fear or nervousness, just a feeling of peace. That's what this woman does to me. She completes me like no one else ever could.

The kittens wake me. It takes me a minute to realize that I fell asleep out here, so I get up with the box still in my hand and head into the bedroom. I see Trinity trying to sit on the edge of the bed, but with her belly, it looks like it's takin' her a while. As I approach her, she turns and smiles, and with that smile, my heart lightens. "You okay, baby? Did ya have a nice nap?"

She pushes her hair back over her shoulders and starts to rub her eyes. "Yes. You wiped my ass out, but I woke up and you weren't here, so I was just coming to find you. Is everything okay?

I can't wait. I know what I want.

Grabbin' both of her hands in mine, I bend down on my knees in front of her so I'm looking her in the eyes when I say this, "Our beginning was shit, and I can never apologize enough for that, but over the last five months, we've built up a friendship again. You are lettin' me back into your life and more importantly back into your heart, you've given me a world I would never want to exist in without you. There's good in this world, Trinity, and for me, that's you. You make me see life in a whole different way with how strong you are and how tough you can be. You have given me a reason to live, and your compassion shows me the way out of those dark days that I have lived in for so long. I want it all, Trinity. I want you as my wife, mother of my children, and guardian of my heart." Reaching down, I pick up the box from the floor and open it to reveal an antique, emerald cut yellow diamond in a platinum band. "This is Des's grandmother's ring. You know my dad took off and Des is more of a dad to me than anything. He wanted me to have this so that I could give it to you so, Trinity Vickers, baby, will you marry me?"

She grasps on to my hands and looks into my eyes

with a smile as big as the sun. "I'd be honored to be your wife and mother of your children. I love you, Cadence Powers. Thank you for loving me back."

I take our hands apart and remove the ring from its box, place it on her finger, and kiss it, giving her a promise, "I'll try hard to never let you down. I love you, baby. I always will."

Pulling her close, I kiss her with all the emotions I'm feelin', and she just gives it right back to me. This is what perfection must feel like.

CHAPTER TWENTY-THREE

CADENCE

It's the week before the charity ride and Wheels & Hogs is frenzied with activity. We all have our normal work, but we also have another job, and that job is to make sure that the ride is a success. On top of that, the property behind the garage is now filling up with people for the final phase of the ride, setting up their tents or campers. Des had Dee order porta-potties that still haven't arrived and as I walk through the front doors, I can hear the frustration in Dee's voice as she speaks to someone on the phone. These are not your cheap shitters. They're the types that have running water, and some even include shower stalls because Des wants to make people as comfortable as possible. I can't believe the number of people who are now here, or on their way. Wolf also has a section of his ranch available for camping. It's on the other side of his property, away from his charity work. He told me he didn't want any issues for the folks he was trying to help. Even those people have stepped up and are involved with trying to assist with the ride as much as they can.

As I head down to Des's office, I think about the last two weeks with Trinity. I've never been so fucking happy in my life as I'm with her and our baby, who will be joining us soon. Wolf and I decided it would be best for her to stay at his place for safety purposes.

I have two surprises for her, and I can't wait to share them with her. The first is that I've turned the guest bedroom closest to the master into a nursery. I even painted it muted shades of yellow, green, and white, which Dee and Willow both helped me pick out, along with a crib and all the other things that the baby will need. Since we don't know the sex of the baby, we picked out clothes that could go either way, so we have something to start with. Archie, Jagger, and Daisy helped me put the shit together and arrange it. A colorful area rug covers the hardwood floors and pretty curtains cover the windows, courtesy of Fern.

Thinking of Fern, the next surprise actually shocked me. Fern and Gabriel are throwin' a surprise baby shower for Trinity and the baby. With all they have going on, they still want to do this, so tomorrow night at the shop, after it closes, is where the shower will be held. Fern was adamant that it be held before the charity ride. I don't like the path her thoughts are taking her in, but I'll do anything Fern asks to make her happy.

Knockin' on Des's door, I wait to hear the gruff,

"*Enter,*" and walk in. Immediately I know that something is up because I see Bear, Stash, Wolf, and some of the MC guys in the office with intense looks on their faces. I look at Des and ask, "What's going on, Des?"

He looks around the room and stops at Wolf, who nods, and then he looks back to me. "Glad you're here, kid. Take a seat cause we've gotta discuss somethin' with you."

As everyone finds somewhere to plop their asses down, I wait for Des to speak, but it's Wolf who starts, "Bro, you know we always have your back, right?"

Something in the back of my mind tells me that I'm not going to like what comes next. "Yeah, I know that Wolf, but what the fuck? Spill it already, will ya?"

Des clears his throat and then reaches across his desk, picks up a picture, and tosses it my way. "Cadence, do you know the man standing next to Trinity's old man, Roman?"

Reaching over the desk, I grab the photo and immediately my stomach clenches. I stand up so abruptly that I knock my chair backward as I yell, "Fuck! It's that motherfucking cocksucker." Losin' the little control, I have; I start pacing and swearing with a wavering voice. I feel light-headed, overheated, and I'm starting to sweat profusely. I'm havin' a goddamn panic attack.

In a flash, Wolf is at my side, grabbing my shoulders and telling me to calm down. I see out of the corner of my eye as Des reaches into his bottom drawer, as Bear brings a glass toward him.

Des pours some liquid into the glass and Bear passes it to Wolf. "Have him drink this. It will help to calm his nerves."

I grab the glass and gulp down the contents. "What the fuck is that? Oh my God, it tastes horrible and burns like fire."

Stash and Bear laugh as they reply at the same time, "Homemade whiskey, kid. We brought it with us. "

After gaining some semblance of control back, I give Wolf a look and he sits down next to me, then I ask Des, "Why do you want to know if I know that guy, Des?"

I wait as Des looks at his watch, then looks back at me. "That man has been asking around town about you, and more specifically, about Trinity and the baby. Knowing what I know from you, I have to ask you, Cadence. Is that Duke?"

Feeling like I can't breathe, my heart feels like it's going to explode. "Little brother, remember you're not alone and I won't allow that asshole to ever hurt you again. Answer Des so we can figure out what we need to do."

Ashamed that my past is coming back to fuck with everyone in my life has me breakin' down. "Yeah, Des. That's Duke. How the fuck does he know Roman Vinkers?" As soon as the words are out of my mouth, I have a flashback and instantly remember how they know each other.

I feel the contraction in my stomach and before I can do anything, I lunge forward as Wolf howls to Des, "Garbage can, he's gonna puke."

Des throws it just as the vomit comes out of my mouth, hitting the rim and rolling down. My shoulders shake uncontrollably as I begin to dry heave while everyone watches in shock. When I'm finally done, Des reaches over with some tissues as Jagger comes in the room with a glass of ice water. "Drink this, Cadence. It might help."

I nod and gulp it down, then tell Jagger, "Thanks, little man. Hey, buddy, do you mind givin' us a few minutes?"

Jagger nods and leaves. I wait until the door is closed before I tell Des, "I didn't even remember him until lookin' at that picture of them together. Roman was one of Duke's 'friends' that joined in on raping me in the cabin."

One of the bikers from the Intruders MC asks me with a look of death in his eyes, "Give me what you got on these people, kid. I'll make sure they're dead before the end of the week, I promise you that. I'll make them suffer for everything they've done. My kid sister was abused, and I can't stand to think of what you've been through. One thing I can't stand is assholes who abuse children."

"Sit down, Enforcer." I watch as Enforcer tries hard to rein in his rage. His hands are clenching as both legs are bouncing in the chair he sits on. He's primed and ready to shoot out of the chair at any minute, but what frightens me the most is the look in his emerald, green eyes. He's thinkin' of his kid sister and wants to hurt anyone who does sick shit like this.

"After they all had their fun with me, Duke dumped me in that back field, probably thinking I was gonna die, which was what I laid out there praying for. I was in really bad shape, and it took months for my body to heal. Doc even had me see a shrink to get my head out of my own ass, and speakin' of my ass, I had to have surgery just to fix all the damage there. Anyway, that guy in the picture is Duke, my stepdad, and that man to his right is Roman Vinkers, my girl's dad, who physically and sexually abused her from the time she was thirteen. He not only sexually abused her, but also pimped her out to his friends, and I don't think I need to go into detail for you. She only shared that part with me recently. So, long-story short, that is Duke, my stepfather who raped me and my brothers, and that there is Roman, Trinity's dad and one of my attackers, also."

As the men seem to be getting more agitated, we all hear a woman gasp right before she screams out, "Oh God, no! Cadence, please tell me it isn't true. My father... he didn't... oh God, no..." Trinity can't finish as she slides to the floor, crying violently. I rush to her side, but she pushes me away, screaming, "Don't touch me! Please don't touch me!"

Doc comes out from behind Trinity and shoves me

out of the way. "What's the matter with her, Doc? Why doesn't she want me to touch her?"

Doc shakes his head. "C, she's going into shock. Don't take it personally, but we just walked in and heard what you said, so she's just discovered that her abuser not only hurt her, but that he participated in abusing and torturing you. Knowing her, she's feeling some guilt and doesn't know what to do. Her mind is fracturing and shutting down to protect her, that's all. Go get Dee or Willow for me, please."

I hurry out of the room, looking for either of the women and can't seem to find them. I do see Archie in the garage workin' on a car, so I rush over to her. "Archie, I need your help. Trinity is in a bad way, and she needs someone that's not me... a woman."

As she turns, I notice how her body tightens up. "What's going on?"

I begin pulling her arm, almost dragging her. "Please, Archie."

As we go down the hall, the sounds coming from Des's office are tearing my heart out. The sounds coming out of the room from Trinity sound like she's completely losing her shit, and that's not good for her or the baby. I'm being pulled back as Archie is trying to pull away from me, appearing not to want to go any farther.

I turn and scream at her, "What the fuck, Archie? It's Trinity. Come on." She comes with me, and we enter the room to see Trinity in Des's office chair with all the men surrounding her. Her eyes are unfocused, and she doesn't even look at me when we enter. Immediately Archie goes to her, shoving men left and right. She sits in front of Trinity, pulling her to her, running her hands down her long, blonde hair. "It's okay, sweetie. Let it out and don't hold back. I'm here and I won't let you go. That's it, baby girl, you just let it all go and for as long as you need to." Suddenly Trinity's arms go around Archie's waist and she starts to wail and cry in a way I've never seen another person do. Didn't even sound human. It sounds like the worst pain coming from your soul, tearing someone apart from the inside. It was breaking my heart to see her like that.

I remember what the doctor said about stress to the mother being stress to the baby, so I begin to make my way to her. Trinity tries to watch me, but her emotions have the best of her right now, so I get down in front of her on my knees. Archie moves and I take her place, but I start to kiss and rub on her belly, feeling the baby movin' around inside of her. The room is quiet, and then I feel hands on my head, holding me close to her belly. Trinity starts running her fingers through my hair and down my neck as I continue to kiss her belly. I start to feel both her and the baby calm physically, but when I look up into her eyes, she tries to look away.

"Trinity, baby. Look at me. Please don't shut me out. I'm the same man you made love to this morning and the same man who loves you more than life itself. Don't let something like this change anything between us, honey. All of that shit is in our past, and it can't hurt us anymore because we have too many amazin' things happening for us, and they will only get better," Tears run down her face, but I continue, "We can't change the past so we have to let it go. Since I found you, I have no reason to go back there. We made it, baby, and we'll continue to make things better, I promise you." I wipe the tears from her face and she stands up, pulling me with her to my feet and reaches around to hug me the best she can with her belly between us.

"I am so sorry for what he did to you... what they both did to you."

I reach down and lift her chin. "You have nothing to be sorry for. *They* hurt us, and we won't allow them to continue. Now, let's sit down and hear what Des has to say about this new piece of news. We need to protect ourselves and our little, tiny peanut."

Once everyone has found a place to sit, Des looks up and then back down at some papers on his desk. "I think we have a situation that is going to need addressing. Both Roman and Duke have been asking questions about the two of you." He looks at Trinity and me. "I have a feelin' they're planning something, and from the type of men they are, we need to be prepared for anything. Kid, can I speak freely?" I look over Trinity's head and nod. "When I found Cadence, he was in such bad shape that I thought he would die on me, but between Doc and Fern, they managed to pull him through. Physically, they had done a number on him, but emotionally and mentally, they had destroyed him." Takin' a minute for that to sink in, Des continues, "I don't think for a minute that Duke is done with Cadence."

My head shoots up to Des. "What the fuck are you talkin' about?"

Des glances at Wolf, who gets up and walks out the door. "Cadence, in about a minute or so, you are going to get very angry at me, but please try to remember that everything I do is for your well-being."

I'm completely confused now as I glance around the room, and it's apparent that everyone but Trinity, Archie, and me are in on whatever is about to go down. Wolf opens the door and as I look behind him, I see my brothers and mother walkin' in, heads hung low. "Holy shit, what are ya all doing here? What the fuck is goin' on?"

Everyone watches in slow motion as my younger brother pushes past Wolf and rushes to me. He grabs me and holds me tightly, outright crying. "Cadence, I missed you so much."

I put my hands around my brother Griffin's shoulders. "Hey, little dude. How have you been doin'?" I then look at my other brother, Ryker, and my mom. Giving both of them a nod, I look to Des. "Care to explain this, boss? Don't get me wrong, I'm happy as hell to see my family but you brought them here for a reason, and it wasn't to just see me, am I right?" I hang tight to Griffin until Jagger comes in with a couple more chairs and bottles of water. I have him sit next to me as everyone gets settled as Des and Wolf stand by the desk.

"We have a situation that's serious as fuck and we need to make sure all are safe. With the charity ride this weekend and all of the stuff that has come to the surface, we need to enlighten all involved. What's said in this room stays in this room, got me?" Des turns to Wolf. "Floor's yours, brother."

Wolf leans on the desk and looks over to my mom and asks, "How well do, or did, you know Duke?"

"I guess as well as anyone knows the person they're with. We were married, so I would say pretty well."

Wolf glares at her. "So did you know he was into human trafficking and slavery?"

She exhales loudly and puts her hand to her chest. "Of course not, Wolf. What are you talking about?"

"I have a young girl at my ranch who was rescued from a horrific situation that both Duke and Roman placed her in, all for fuckin' money."

Now this has everyone's attention because Wolf is usually the quiet one and never swears in front of women. He softly apologizes to the ladies and continues, "We have been led to believe that they are looking to kidnap Trinity and the baby to sell on their black market. The baby is spoken for already; being sold for close to six figures, while Trinity is their biggest demand. A young woman, blonde hair, blue eyes; she's worth a mint to them." Wolf looks to Trinity. "Your father was priming you for this. That was his plan all along, but once we took you, it pissed him off because his payday was gone."

Trinity shakes in my arms. "How do you know all of this, and can we even believe it's true?"

Wolf looks at her sadly. "Besides Pru, at my ranch, identifying both men, we had an inside connection."

Now I'm pissed. "Who is this insider, and why am I just hearin' about this now? What the fuck else have you and Des been hiding from me? I am not a fuckin' kid, but a grown-ass man, dammit," I yell.

Wolf nods to Bear, who opens the door and lets in Axe, Wolf's brother. I immediately look to Des because he doesn't like Axe, but to my surprise, Des walks up to Axe and gives him a fist bump. "This here is my brother, Axe. He is part of the Native Warrior Riders. What no one knows is that as bad as these fuckers are," he glares at his brother, "they are all undercover police officers, FBI, and DEA. That is what their membership is made of."

Axe wastes no time. "Just to give everyone the basics, these guys are really bad, and their associates have no conscience. We pulled Pru and a couple of others from men who had bought them as sex slaves. I can't begin to tell you what these women have been through, but I digress. All we know is that for the last month, you two have been followed wherever you go. They're getting your routines down so they can grab Trinity when you least expect it. They've a house on the outskirts of the next town over so they'll probably wait until the baby is born so he, or she, can be sold, and they can prepare and train Trinity before transporting her to her owner."

At this point, I am livid. "What the fuck have you been doin' if they have this already planned? Were you just waiting for them to grab her?" I can hear the terror of that scenario in my voice.

"Cadence don't take this the wrong way, but without us on this, she would have already been gone. We've been messing with their people, pulling them over for stupid shit, always stopping them in some way when they seem too close." Turning to Trinity he asks her, "Remember when you were at Wolf's last week and that van approached the house? Did you see it take off as soon as Wolf and Des showed on their bikes? We called the boys to get there ASAP. We were there if it went wrong, but we are tryin' to keep our presence low key and not give away what we know... yet. So, now let's discuss why we have pulled Cadence's family in too. It was leaked that Duke had a connection in the service that was gonna get his gang to bully Ryker, and when we say bully, we don't just mean call him names and pick on him. These are hard-core motherfuckers who take pleasure in other people's pain. We couldn't let that happen, so we pulled him in with your mom and younger brother and brought them to Wolf's. They are staying in one of the cabins in the back, Cadence, and they're safe. We've that whole area under surveillance, twenty-four seven. Now with the charity ride this weekend, we believe that's the time they're gonna use to kidnap Trinity. With everyone's attention concentrated on the ride, they believe it will be an easy pick. Our job is to not only make sure the ride goes off without a hitch, but protect both of you, Cadence." Taken aback by Axe's willingness to help us, I'm speechless.

Des takes over. "The ride is still going on, so I suggest you all keep a mindful watch of the people around you and where you're at all times. Don't do anything alone, do you understand? I'm also askin' every one of you to spread the word about checkin' in with the Bone Marrow Foundation. I don't care if you have to talk to every single person on this ride, you make sure everyone knows how easy it is and where they can be tested. We need as many people as possible to find this match for Fern, and for others."

"I want to be tested to see if I can help Fern, Doc. How do I do that?" Griffin asks. Doc looks at Griffin and begins to tear up but puts on a bright smile as he begins to explain to Griffin the procedure.

Axe steps up to us. "We've a plan and will fill everyone in. Please just go about your normal routines and don't anyone try to be a hero. Concentrate on the charity ride and we will cover the rest. Cadence, Trinity, can I've a minute of your time?"

CHAPTER TWENTY-FOUR

TRINITY

"Okay, kids. It's like this. Both Duke and Roman are in some deep shit and you two are their ticket out."

I look confused and ask, "What do you mean, Axe? How can we possibly help them out with whatever trouble they're in? We don't have money or expensive shit, so how can we get them out of a jam?"

"You have the most important item for them to sell. They have a buyer for your baby, and the money from that sale will take care of their debts with the human traffickers, or at least bring them current."

"Promise me that no matter what happens, you'll not let them get my baby. You can't let Roman touch my baby, no matter what. He's already fucked up my life and I refuse to give him the chance to do that to another innocent child. Please, Axe, Cadence, promise me. I don't care about my life, just protect my baby." I start to lose my shit again, crying uncontrollably when Des bursts through the door, concern on his face.

"Sweetie, you need to calm down. You know this isn't good for the baby, so come on, Trinity. Take a deep breath." My attention is so focused on Des that I don't see Doc come around the back to give me a shot. I'm shocked and scream at Doc, askin' what he just did to me, but then I begin to feel tired and my body starts to relax and get soft, so Cadence grabs me and lifts me into his arms, carrying me out of the room. Axe just shakes his head as Doc and Des both demand to know what's going on.

~Des~

Axe gives the abbreviated version to Doc and me, explaining the plan to protect both Trinity and the baby. Doc walks out of the room, and I look point blank at Axe and says, "Do you believe the bullshit you just told us? Because personally, I think we're about to have a disaster on our hands, and right in the middle of the fucking charity ride that I've been involved with for the last nine months of my life. So tell me how you can guarantee her safety, when you don't even know why those two assholes are in trouble in the first place. And to top that off, you don't know who put in a bid to buy an unborn baby. Why should I have faith in you, Axe? To make myself very clear, I really can't stand you and I certainly don't trust you."

"I know your feelings regarding me Des, but this isn't about us, it's about an innocent woman and her child. My promise to you is that I will risk my own life to protect Trinity. Knowin' the backstory of both those kids, it tears my fuckin' heart out, so you can hate and despise me you Bastard, but either work with me or stay the fuck out of my way. I don't care which way you go, asshole. My main objective is to protect those two kids in there and their baby." I take a minute to think about what he said, and then I nod my head in agreement.

~Cadence~

I put Trinity to bed in her room at Wolf's. She's fighting sleep and losing the battle due to the shot that Doc gave her, "Baby, close your eyes and try to sleep. Nothing is gonna happen; I swear that to you on my life."

Her hold on me tightens for a moment, then I feel her body relax and she seems to let sleep take her as I hear her soft snores. I lie down next to her and let the entire situation hit me. Once again, there are men tryin' to fuck with my life, but this time it includes the woman I love and my unborn child. Caressing her back and listening to her breathing softly in her drug-induced sleep, I promise to whomever hears my solemn oath that I will die for the two most important people in my life, who also happen to be in my arms at this moment.

After what seems like forever, I feel my body relax and finally close my eyes, only to drift off to a restless sleep.

CHAPTER TWENTY-FIVE

CADENCE

With all the bullshit going on, I didn't think I'd sleep, but fuck I did. Slowly opening my eyes, I feel her warmth next to me. She is so close to my side that I can feel her exhaled little snores on my skin. Not that I'm complaining, because I'm not. This woman, who has control of my Goddamn heart, has been able to do something no one else has ever been able to do—give me hope.

Knowing the next couple of days are going to be full of stress, I tighten my arm around her, just takin' in this moment. I feel a push into my side and realize it's the baby kicking. He, or she, moves around a lot. I take a deep pull of air through my nostrils and let it out through my open mouth. These breathing techniques have helped me through a lot of shit. Time and time again as I do this, I feel the baby kicking my side, and then I feel the tears running down my face because I'm so fuckin' overwhelmed by how much love I have for these two.

I know she's awake before she says a word. Lookin' down at her as she raises her head and our eyes meet. Leaning toward her, I rub my nose against hers then give her a soft kiss on her full lips. "Mornin' beautiful. How're you feeling?"

Stretching her body, she mutters, "Okay, I guess. This kid is kicking the crap out of me for Pete's sake."

I chuckle as I sit up. "Baby, our *little, tiny peanut* was kicking my side while you slept."

"What's on the agenda for today?" she asks, as she tries to rock out of bed with no success. She's gotten so big in the front that she can barely walk without tilting. "Come on, give me a handout of this bed. Quit staring at me and help me," she growls. Trinity trying to sound all badass has me chuckling under my breath as I give her a hand.

After we get out of bed and do our morning routines, we both head down to the kitchen, hand in hand. As we approach the kitchen, we hear angry voices and muffled moans.

We run into the kitchen, not sure if Wolf or someone else is hurt, but what we find is Wolf zipping his jeans and buckling up his belt. Wolf turns around, shocked. I look to the back door and see a figure with long, reddish brown hair walking quickly past the window with her head down, going toward the back forty where he has all the cabins for his sheltered folks.

For a while the three of us just stare at each other,

no one knowing what to say. Finally, I look at Wolf. "Remember you have to bring Trinity to the garage after hours tonight. She's spendin' the night with me, okay?" Wolf shakes his head in agreement. Wolf and I both know tonight is the surprise shower for Trinity. Today is Wednesday, so we only have tomorrow and Friday before we start the weekend of events for the charity ride.

"Do either of you want some coffee?"

"Sure, baby. I'd love a cup of joe." I know that now is not the time to question Wolf, but it is coming soon.

~Trinity~

As Wolf and I head toward the garage, I attempt to make conversation. Since this morning, things have been awkward. "Wolf, are you upset with me for something?"

"Little one, I could never be mad at you. There's so much goin' on that my mind is all over the place. Sorry to be such bad company." After a pause, we continue to talk and joke all the way to the garage.

As we enter the parking lot, I notice how dark it is inside, "Wonder why there are no lights on. Guess everyone is gone for the day."

"Hang on, Trinity. Just give me a minute. I've got to

check my phone." Wolf finishes his text, gets out of the truck, and rounds the front to help me down.

Grabbing the handle of the door, Wolf guides me in with his hand on my back through the dark entrance. Suddenly the lights come on and a loud "Surprise" knocks me back into Wolf. Watching everyone come to greet me, I finally get what's going on. They are throwing me a baby shower. Cadence comes around and puts his arm around my waist, pulling me tight to his body. The smile on his face brings such joy to my heart, and so does this new family of mine.

Fern, assisted by Doc, approaches Cadence and me with a huge smile on her face. Gently cupping my face in her hands, she kisses my cheek. "Trinity, we wanted to make sure you had a proper baby shower for that little one so come in, say hi to everyone, and let's eat and have some baby fun."

"You all planned a baby shower for me? But you've already done so much for me. I have no words to express how I feel for all of you."

Dee Dee comes around. "Honey, you are the sweetest thing that has come into our family. Now that you and Cadence are getting married and having a baby, we're now all your family. You're stuck with us, so let's eat and open presents."

Finally, Cadence's mom approaches me, hesitantly. "I'm so thrilled for both of you and happy that I'm able to be here to celebrate this happy occasion with you."

Looking up at her son with wet eyes, she tries to say

something, but Cadence puts his arms around her, pulling her close. "I know, Mom. It's okay, I know."

She puts her head on his chest, wrapping her arms around him. "I am so sorry, Cadence, for everything."

He nods and whispers in her ear "We'll talk, but not now. This is a happy time and both Trinity and I are glad that you're here to help celebrate your grandchild, okay?"

Cadence and I sit in the middle of the room as Daisy, Archie, and Willow bring gifts to for us to open. From Daisy and Jagger, we receive a basket full of baby necessities. Willow and Archie give us a Pack-and Go. Surprising the both of us, the MCs got together and purchased a stroller, car seat, diaper bag filled with all kinds of things, and a gift card to Babies R Us for a whopping five hundred dollars. I'm beyond shocked. Des and Dee purchased a rocking chair and ottoman for the baby's room, along with a bassinet for our room to keep the baby in the first couple of weeks. Cadence's mom's gifts are a handmade knitted blanket, along with some cute outfits. Besides that, as we open the box, I take in a deep breath as Cadence lifts a Christening gown out of the box. Looking at his mom, she tells him softly, "Yes, that is the same gown your brothers and you were christened in."

When we get to Wolf's gift, we're both totally shocked. He's carved us a rocking horse for the baby. He also gives us some handmade rattles and toys, but the one gift that takes our breath away is the beautiful dream catcher he's made for the baby's room.

While Wolf, Willow, Archie, and Axe carry the gifts up the stairs, I thank each and every one of my new family for everything they've done. Cadence finally drags me away and takes me into his apartment, where he proceeds to take me down the hall to the spare bedroom, right next to the master. I notice the door is closed, which is strange because he leaves all the doors open for the kittens. He grabs the door handle and as he opens it, he whispers in my ear, "Surprise, baby." The room is dark until he hits the light switch. Holy shit, I'm blown away as I look at the once plain spare bedroom. It's been turned into a nursery. The room is packed with everything from tonight, along with a crib, dresser, and a changing table, but what catches my eye are the murals all over the walls. Tiny baby animals are placed around the entire room, along with some Native American signs or symbols. As I walk to the crib, I can actually feel my heart beating faster. Without even asking, I know that Fern made the bedding. The sheets, the pillowcase, and the small comforter are all made from a material with baby animals on it. At the foot of the bed is a crocheted blanket in the same colors as the room. It's so overwhelming, and I'm going on emotional overload. Cadence Powers did all of this for me. I know deep in my heart that no matter what happens in the future, I'll never forget this moment that he has given me.

"I love it, Cadence. It's absolutely perfect. Our baby is so lucky to have you for a daddy."

"Baby, I am so glad you like it. This was a team

effort. Fern, Dee, Willow, Archie, and even the kids helped."

As we enjoy the peace and quiet of the moment, suddenly we hear loud voices coming down the hallway. "Dude, where do you want the rest of this shit? Got stuff to do." I watch as Cadence shudders at Enforcer's words. Who would have thought a badass biker who kills people and enjoys it also wanted to be a part of the baby shower, even volunteering to bring all the presents up here?

Cadence calls to them, "Back here. We're in the nursery." As the evening continues on, everyone works on getting the gifts put into their proper places within the nursery. When everything is done, everyone heads out, probably seeing that I'm just beat.

"Baby, go on and get ready for bed. I'm gonna finish some stuff for the ride and then I'll be in, okay?" I nod and head to the bedroom.

~Cadence~

I go to the office and pull out the folders to confirm everything I'm responsible for is done and in place. Tomorrow is Thursday and it starts the arrival of all the people who planned on participating in the charity ride. I know the townsfolk are enjoying the added income all the visitors are already startin' to bring in.

I'm in charge of sign-in and registration for the ride. Also, since I live above the garage, I'm in charge of everyone camping behind Connelly's Garage, making sure it all runs smoothly. Even as I sit here in the office, there're campers already on the property. This is going to be a busy weekend, and on top of that, I'm still worried about the situation with Roman and Duke. I'd to trust that my family and friends, including Axe, are gonna be able to protect Trinity and the baby. They're my top priority.

CHAPTER TWENTY-SIX

CADENCE

It's finally Saturday, the day of the Charity Ride for Fern, with work startin' bright and early. Everyone is runnin' their asses off, trying to keep all the shit together and tight, and more importantly, running smoothly. A couple of small issues needed to be taken care of, like where the bikers were going to fuel up on the ride. Des, Bear, and Stash ran the course last night and marked the fuel stops. Besides that, the event is going off without a hitch. All the women are havin' fun as the kids run around, making a mess of things.

I'm busy headin' up the table for registration and sign-up, while Trinity is close by with the ladies at the bakery tables. She has spent the last day and a half baking everything you could think of in Wolf's kitchen. Watchin' her from afar, I'm in such awe of her. She's almost nine months pregnant and ready to deliver our baby but still in the thick of things.

Gettin' my head back into the game, I call the next

in line so they can register. I look over to where Jagger is sitting and smile at the young man. He has grown over the last couple of months, filling in and bulking up. Quiet as ever, Jagger works with a sense of responsibility of a much older guy. Never losin' his temper with the bikers, his line seems to continually move faster than mine. This day can't end fast enough for me.

As it gets closer to the "first bike out" time, Wolf, Des, and I go to the shop to grab our bikes. We take that little bit of time to bullshit on the way to the garage and laugh about silly shit that has happened with this charity ride.

Wolf and Des will be leading the ride, while Enforcer and I will bring up the end. With all of the shit we have to do, we managed to find time to work on our own bike's, so the machines are in top shape for this ride.

Each of our bikes are custom and built to each man's specifications. Des's Panhead is a brilliant cherry red, while Wolf's Fat Boy is a sapphire blue with silver flames. My Shovelhead is matte black with lots of chrome.

Once we get them out of the garage, we lock everything down and start to head back to the parking lot where the ride starts. My phone vibrates on my side and at first I ignore it, but as it continues, I get a horrible feeling deep in my gut. I motion for the guys with my phone that I've got to pull over and stop, and they point to their phones as well. We pull over and I kick my bike in neutral. I check my texts at the same time as both Des and Wolf do. Knowin' shit is about to go down, I look at the text, at the same time I hear Des start to scream and swear, "Fuckin' motherfucker! When I catch those two assholes, they're dead, and I mean after I pull their limbs off and stuff their dicks down their throats, dead."

Meanwhile, Wolf is tryin' to make a call as his hands shake. Looking at the screen on my phone, the text is from Axe and it reads, *"Where the fuck are all of you? Duke and Roman just grabbed Trinity, Dee Dee, and Willow. Get your asses back here right fuckin' now!"*

I feel like my world is turnin' upside down. My entire body burns with rage as my breathing becomes shallow, makin' it damn near impossible to swallow. With all three of us gone, that left the girls vulnerable. Fuck! Those bastards have her. They have Trinity and the others. Time to kick some major ass.

CHAPTER TWENTY-SEVEN

DEE DEE

Willow and I are handcuffed to the bench along the wall of a portable medical vehicle. We watch in horror as Roman and a woman in full medical garb strap Trinity to the gurney. She doesn't look good at all. She's extremely pale and I can see that her breathing is shallow, and her pupils are dilated as she stares at her father in horror. As he tightens the strap around her shoulders, he grabs her breast, squeezing hard. "Damn, girl. You should have never kept this tight body away from me. Your tits have grown, and you actually look like a real woman that I could totally fuck hard.

I take in an aggravated gasp of air. "Get your fucking hands off her, you sick son-of-a-bitch. Once Des and Cadence find you, they will tear you apart you old limp dick."

Roman walks toward the bench and backhands me right into Willow. Blood shoots out of the split in my lip. "Shut the fuck up, you old whore. You aren't worth much but we'll take what we can get, that is after we break you in, you mouthy bitch. Gonna learn what that mouth should be used for."

After grabbing his crotch, he then turns his attention to Willow. "Now you, bitch, are worth a mint. It'll be fun fuckin' you into submission and showin' you how to treat real man." Willow shifts so both of us are huddled together. I watch nervously as Roman runs his hands along her sides up to her breasts. He leans in and smells her neck. "Damn, bitch. You smell good enough to eat." As he starts to laugh, we realize that the vehicle has come to a complete stop.

The double back doors open up as Duke steps in and turns to pull them closed behind him. "What the fuck? Why haven't you started yet? We don't have a lot of time." He glares at Trinity and then her swollen pregnant belly. "Let's start this shit and get that fucking brat out of her. We have people waitin' for that kid and their patience has run out." Trinity starts to shake while swinging her head right to left as both Willow and I begin screaming, kicking, anything and everything that we can possibly do. Duke walks over to us and grabs our hair by the roots to get us to shut up. "Bitches, shut your motherfuckin' mouths or I'll deal with both of you right now. Won't be able to scream you heads off if I you're your tongues out. Your decision. We take the fucking brat, or I fuck you raw and put a bullet in your brains. Time is ticking."

As Willow and I quiet down, we watch the woman working with these deranged assholes start placing instruments on a rolling table by Trinity's side. I know this is going from bad to worse as the medic grabs a large needle, explaining to the two men, "We need to get her up and bent over so I can give her the epidural shot."

Roman goes around and loosens the straps, "Behave, you little whore, or you'll pay, do you hear me?" Trinity looks like a doll with her arms hanging at her sides, her body limp and lifeless. Both Roman and Duke take a side and bend her over so the needle-baring medic can administer the shot. We watch in shock as the woman feels around Trinity's back then swabs it down before grabbing the syringe. She whispers in Trinity's ear, "Sweetheart, you need to stay really still. First, it will feel like a pop, and then it will get really warm. Just try to remain completely still." Trinity is violently shaking but takes a breath and somehow manages to stay still. Her hands are clenched into fists as the needle enters her back. It takes just a few seconds and then they lay her back down.

As the medic starts to drape a gown over her, Roman says, "No clothes or drapes. We want to make sure nothing goes wrong."

I plead for Trinity's baby, "Please don't do this. With the stress you've put on her, the baby could be in jeopardy. What kind of sick deranged fucks are you to cut a child from its mother? And you, you bitch. Wait until I get my hands on you."

The men look at each other and laugh loudly. "We could give a fuck what you think, slut. This baby is worth one hundred fifty thousand to us on the black market. We need that to pay back some overdue debts or be put six feet under, but what we get for all of you when we're done with you will make us enough to live comfortably for the rest of our lives away from here. Far, far away from here."

~Trinity~

As I listen to the conversation around me, I know something is off. The woman/medic didn't strap me back down after the shot, she just laid the straps over me. Neither handcuffs, nor zip ties, were ever placed on my wrists. Then to my complete surprise, the medic placed a very small gun in my palm and closed my fingers over it. When I glance at her, she mouthed one word, "Axe."

My heartbeat increases and I feel an anxiety come over my entire body. Oh my God, she's one of Axe's people. She's risking her life to help all of us. I try to relax a little as it hits me that Axe has someone working undercover watching over and having our backs. Thank God she knows what she's doing.

Both men approach the gurney as Duke questions the medic, "Why haven't you started pulling the kid out of her? Don't be tryin' to pull anything over on us, because I'll put a bullet in your head."

"My name is Paula and I'm a nurse practitioner and have done this procedure multiple times. If we all work together, no one will get—"

Before she even finishes, Roman whacks her in the back of her head with his fist. "Once again, know your place, bitch. We're running this show, not you. Do what you're told, and you might walk away breathin'."

Paula looks first at Roman, and then at Duke. "I can't start until the epidural is working. She still has feeling down below her waist, see?" She reaches below the sheet and squeezes my thigh. Even though I don't feel a thing, I let out a squeal and jerk my body.

The men watch closely. "How much more time do you need?" Duke asks angrily.

"Probably ten more minutes, if that," Paula replies as someone's phone goes off.

Both men jump as Roman pulls his phone from his pocket, motioning Duke to leave the vehicle. "Bitches, we'll be right outside so don't try anything funny because there are consequences to everything you do goin' forward. Got it?" Dee and Willow nod as Paula is going through some protocol with me.

As the men slam the doors, we hear a lock and Paula softly whispers, "We don't have a lot of time, so please listen. I'm working with Axe and they have a tracking device on this vehicle, and one on me, so it's only a matter of time before they find us. We need to be prepared." She approaches Dee Dee and Willow and pulls a black bag from her back pocket. As she opens it, I notice it has tools in it. In a matter of minutes, she opens the cuffs and cuts the plastic from their hands and feet.

"Sorry about threatening you earlier," Dee says as Paula nods.

Paula reaches into the overhead, moving things this way and that and pulls out a gray object and hands it to Willow. "This is a Taser, so if we need to protect ourselves when one of them gets close, just touch them with this and they will go down." Moving to Dee, she hands her a gun. "Please hide this in the back of your jeans. Only use it if you have to." We all hear the lock being opened and resume our prior positions.

As the men enter, Paula is setting up a tray with multiple surgical instruments on it. She pinches me and asks, "Do you feel that?"

I shake my head and reply, "Barely, but I can still feel it."

Paula turns to the men. "We should be able to begin in five minutes. As we wait, I will need the water I asked you to supply. Can you tell me where it is?"

Both men look dumbfounded, and then at each other. "Did you get the water?" Roman asks as Duke just shakes his head.

Paula gives them a look. "This baby is your meal ticket and I need the water to clean the brat when I get it out of her, not to mention, you can't afford for her to get an infection. There are too many people in here as it is, so let's try to keep the possibility of problems to a minimum, all right?"

As the men argue about who is gonna get water,

Paula gives all the women a look as she reaches into her front pocket, glancing at her phone, places it back into her pocket, then nods toward Dee Dee and Willow with a strange look and smile on her face. She locks eyes with me and mouths, "There, there, sweetie. You hang on."

As she moves around the interior, I notice that she's placing all the machinery right in front of her, separating her from the men. She squeezes my hand with the small gun then looks at me. "Be ready sweetie."

As the men push the double doors open to go get water, it all happens so fast that I'm not sure what is going on. I watch in horror as someone grabs Duke's arm and pulls him from the vehicle, throwing him roughly to the concrete. As Roman turns to move back into the vehicle, Axe appears at the doors, leaping in and grabbing Roman from behind in a stranglehold. As they struggle, Roman pulls the gun from his belt and aims it toward me with a crazy look on his face. "Little whore. You've been a fuckin' thorn in my ass for too long. Burn in hell with your momma." He pulls the trigger at the same time Paula jumps in front of me on the bed. The force of falling and then landing heavily across me, it takes my breath away.

Struggling to remove Paula from lying over me, I hear her moan. Reaching to touch her, I feel something wet and look at my hand that's covered in Paula's blood. Oh my God. She saved our lives.

I start to go into shock. My body is trembling as I

feel my limbs go numb and my heart begins to beat erratically. My vision is going blurry and my throat is closing up. Feeling someone moving Paula off me, the air whooshes back into my lungs, giving me a moment of relief as I hungrily take in a much-needed breath. Trying to focus my eyes on who is standing to my side holding my clammy hand, I can finally see that it's Axe. His eyes are watching me closely as his hand is gently rubbing my wrist. His closeness is having a strange effect on me, making me feel safe and protected. I give Axe a small smile of gratitude and he gives me back a head nod before handing me off to another person as he goes to check on Paula, who is being treated by way too many people.

Dee Dee and Willow rush over in the cramped area, both grabbing a hand and gently helping me off the gurney. Immediately my head swims and I get dizzy. Feeling like I'm about to pass out, I grab Dee's hand, telling her, "No matter what happens, take care of my little baby. Please, Dee Dee. Promise me that you'll always take care of Cadence and the baby." As Dee screams for help, I slide from their hands onto the floor as my legs crumble beneath me from the effects of the epidural.

CHAPTER TWENTY-EIGHT

CADENCE

Hearing Dee screaming has me pushing my way through a crowd of police, MC members, paramedics, and God knows who else. Even with my strength, I just can't get close enough. I can feel my frustration growing until I finally lose it. "Get the fuck out of the way, every fuckin' one of you, *MOVE*! My fiancée and baby are in there and they need me for Christ's sake. I said move your asses now!" As multiple heads turn in my direction, I hear Willow calling my name loudly.

As I approach the vehicle, I see a woman covered in blood being worked on by a ton of people, and she doesn't look good. I feel a presence and look up to see Axe watching closely as they continue to work on the woman. From what I can see from the emotions crossing his face, he knows the woman, and he knows her very well.

Willow sticks her head out. "Cadence, get up here now. Trinity's in trouble. Come on, C, she needs you."

As I push past Axe, I turn and grab his shoulders and quietly mumble, "Thanks, bro. I owe you. In fact, I'm in your debt for the rest of my life." Axe looks directly into my eyes for a minute and nods before he turns back to his friend.

Once I get inside the medical vehicle, I see Trinity propped up on the table with both Dee and Willow beside her as a paramedic is working on her. I rush over to her side as Willow moves to stand next to Dee Dee. "Baby? Oh shit, please baby be okay. Come on now, we're in the home stretch, sugar, so don't do this now." As I look down, I see blood pooling at her feet.

"Motherfucker, she's bleedin'. Someone fuckin' help her. It's the baby, isn't it?" As more paramedics come in to help, they push all three of us out of the way. One is checking her pulse; one is putting oxygen on her face as the other is listening intently to her belly. We all hold our breath, waiting to see what is going on with Trinity.

As we watch, her eyes slowly start to flicker open. She looks dumbfounded for a minute then glances toward me, starting to break down into uncontrollable sobs. As I watch, her head starts to move repeatedly from side to side and her eyes start to get glassy, then start to glaze over. She starts to hyperventilate as the medic ups the oxygen.

The medics are advising her to breathe deeply but they are getting nowhere. I push them out of the way, grabbin' her cheeks, forcing her eyes to mine. "Baby, calm the fuck down now. Ya have to relax because every time you get upset, it upsets our baby. Please, Trinity, listen to these people. They know what they're doin'." I start to gently caress her face then move on down to her shoulders with soft pressure. She lets out a sigh and seems to sink into the gurney. I continue to massage her arms, hands, and temples until she finally starts to calm down.

As I watch the medics, they all look up to me after trying to locate the blood running down her leg. "Sir, the blood is from a cut on her thigh. It isn't the baby."

I feel as if the world tilts at his words, as I stroke her hair. "Trinity, our baby is okay and safe. Thank God!"

As she nods toward me, all of a sudden I hear a thunderous sound that almost shakes the vehicle. Trinity grabs my hand. "Oh my gosh, what's that?"

I turn to the door then back at her with a huge smile. "Baby, you feel strong enough to stand?" She shakes her head no so I pick her up in my arms and carry her to the doors. Pushin' them open, she gasps. For as far as our eyes can see are motorcycles. Both sides of the street are packed with bikes as they come to a stop about a half a block away from where we are watchin'. I continue to hold her close as we see through the center Wolf's huge truck making its way slowly toward us. Once the truck stops, Trinity and I watch as Doc steps down from the passenger side and opens the back door. He reaches in and gently lifts Fern out. He starts to walk in our direction when we watch her squeeze his arms and say something in his ear. He shakes his head but she squeezes again. He stops and very carefully puts her feet down on the street. He waits for her to steady herself and they walk slowly toward we are. When they reach us, Fern reaches out for Trinity. "How are you doing, honey? Is everything okay?" Trinity shakes her head grabbing on to Fern's hand and squeezing tightly. Doc comes up behind his wife, just as she seems to lose what little strength she has left.

The bikes are idling in the background like thunder when all of a sudden, a dirt bike comes up around Wolf's truck with Jagger and Daisy on the back. When the kid stops suddenly and shuts the bike off, they both jump off and run screaming, "Mom, Mom! Where're you? Are you okay? Mom?"

Dee Dee sticks her head out, looking at her children with a serene smile on her face until she sees the bike in the middle of the street, "Jagger Holden, please tell me you didn't ride that thing here?" He just shrugs his shoulders and runs grabbin' her and pulling her close in a hug. Daisy comes up on the side of her brother and gets in on the hug also. Des approaches them and Daisy grabs his hand, pulling him into the family hug.

"If everyone is okay, we need to get the charity ride going. All these bikers wouldn't leave until they knew that Trinity, Dee Dee, and Willow were safe. Can we tell them all is good so we can finally get this underway?" Wolf says with a smile.

As Wolf makes an announcement to all the bikers waiting, he also reminds them to stop by the kiosks and get checked while Fern and Doc stand at his side. "Now let's get back to the starting line so we can get this ride started." All the bikers start revving up their engines until the sound is so fucking loud that the earth throbs under my feet.

~Des~

It's been a long day for everyone. Between the excitement with Duke and Roman to the Charity Ride for Fern, then the party after, the entire group is exhausted. As I look around at my crew, I see Trinity slumped against Cadence on a picnic bench, passed out, while Cadence runs his fingers through her hair, keeping a watchful eye on the crowd. Across from them at the same table are Dee Dee, Jagger, and Daisy, all talking and drinking sodas. To the side of the table Willow, Archie, Bear, Stash, and Enforcer are sitting in the grass, talking, and laughing. Even Cadence's mother and two brothers seem to be enjoying themselves. There is gonna be a lot of work there to get the Powers family back together and emotionally healthy.

All around me are groups of townsfolk, MC members, riders, cops, and Axe's people, just relaxin' and enjoying the beautiful evening, listening to the band that's playing in the park. I spot Deputy George with a couple of his guys just walkin' through, making sure there is no trouble.

Feeling eyes on me, I continue to look around until I hit a pair of aqua eyes staring intently at me. Raising my eyebrows at Axe, I return the stare. Finally, Axe leisurely heads toward me, lookin' this way and that way before he gets to me.

"You did well, Desmond. Really well. From what I've heard, just about everyone has been to the kiosk to be tested, so even if they don't help Fern, they will help someone, which is just fuckin' amazing. Tomorrow I'll need to talk to the people involved with this whole situation involvin' the two assholes Duke and Roman. We need to get all the details straight, so we make sure those two fuckers are locked up for a long time. Hopefully, they will lead us to the ones runnin' the human trafficking/sex trade ring."

"How's your girl that got injured?"

Axe's head spins. "What do you mean, *my girl*. We work together, Desmond, that's it."

"Dude, I was just asking how she was doing, that's all, so calm the fuck down."

Axe takes a breath and gazes over the crowd. "She went into surgery about two hours ago. I waited until they told me she was out and everything went well. Paula will be out of commission for a while, but thank God, she'll pull through."

As the evening turns into night, Axe and I watch

the sun set and the people start to thin as the benefit for Fern and Doc winds down. I feel like a weight has been removed from my shoulders, realizing that all the work we've put into this paid off in more ways than I could have ever imagined.

CHAPTER TWENTY-NINE

TRINITY

The day after the ride was extremely busy for Dee Dee, Willow, and I. We all had to give statements regarding to what actually happened in the mobile medical unit. With our combined statements and the report filed after my altercation with Roman at the doctor's office, the police were sure that neither man would be let out on bail and would be held until their trials started. The more I found out about these two criminals, the more I came to realize how lucky the baby and I were.

Roman and Duke rolled over on their bosses, so those men were either dead or being picked up and arrested. Their victims were already coming forward once they were freed from the grips of their captors. With Roman and Duke ratting out their contacts, Axe was sure the head of the whole operation was already taking care of business, getting rid of anyone who could lead back to him. Apparently he was in the process of doing just that, authorities were already finding some dead bodies, and that would eventually include Roman and Duke.

Axe and his team would have their work cut out for them now, since they had no leads or witnesses to who the asshole leader of this organization was.

~Cadence~

After the incident with Roman and Duke, both Trinity and I sat down with Fern, Doc, and my mother, Ruthie. I listened as Fern explained to Trinity and me that since these latest occurrences, we should make sure to talk to our therapists about it all, which we both intend to do. Therapy has helped Trinity and I so much over the months, and it was helpin' me tremendously since I really began opening up and telling my whole story and being honest about everything goin' on in my life. We're also seeing therapists individually, and also a couples' therapist together. It was a lot of time to put in, but it's worth it to us.

I wasn't lookin' forward to admitting that Trinity's father, Roman, was one of the many men who abused me that time with Duke, but I was ready to talk about it so I could begin to move past it and move forward with my family. I didn't want this hangin' over our heads any more than it already was.

Trinity, on the other hand, has bounced back like a

fuckin' gymnast. She likes her counselor a lot and has been able to open up easily. I can see her finding her inner peace, and she's just as ready to move past this and start our lives together, baggage free, so to speak.

Feeling Trinity start to wake, I pull her into my arms and nuzzle up against the back of her neck. I love the smell of her and would inhale her scent whenever I can. I can't get enough of her. As she squirms closer to me, her back to my front, my cock hardens immediately. She pushes her ass into me and giggles. Reachin' around, I tweak her nipple and listen to her squeal, as I continue to push my erection against her ass, makin' me moan. "Baby, you keep rubbing your ass on my cock, we won't be getting out of this bed anytime soon."

She reaches around and grabs my cock with a firm grip. "You can get up, Cadence. No one is tying you to the bed." I take her nipple in between my two fingers and pull until it's swollen and plump.

She's now startin' to breathe hard as I lean in and speak into her ear, "If you want to be tied to the bed, just tell me. I'm up for anything darlin'. You know that." She shivers in anticipation as I slowly reach my hand back and grab the cheeks of her ass, massaging it and puttin' my fingers close to her back hole.

Now moaning loudly, Trinity is trying to move her hand on my cock but being extremely pregnant is makin' it hard for her to move where she needs to. I can feel her frustration and get out of bed. I reach for her and help her to a sitting position. I grab all the pillows and place them in front of the headboard, then help her sit directly in front so that she is half lying down. I put one leg over a pillow, so it spreads her wide for me. This position gives me access to everything I want.

I run my finger from her back hole to her clit. She shivers as I continue to do this while spreadin' her increasing wetness both to the back and to the front around her sensitive clit. "Baby, please. I need you to really touch me. I need to feel it deep inside. Please." I chuckle as I put pressure on her with my fingers and start to roll her swollen clit between them occasionally giving it a squeeze. She's moving her hips back and forth, trying to increase the pressure but to no avail.

I'm controlling everything. Knowin' she needs more, I separate her wet lips and push two fingers deep into her tight, hot pussy. I can feel the tremors deep inside her begin as I start the motion of going in and out, adding more pressure each time. As she gets even wetter, I hook my fingers, feeling for the bundle of nerves hidden deep inside of her. When I find it, I start to rub back and forth on the spot, watching as she falls apart. She's moanin' and squirmin' as I keep at her clit repeating the same pattern of rubbing back and forth, then pushing down hard before squeezing the puffed bundle of nerves. Hearing her fighting' to catch her breath, I take my other hand and place a finger directly on her back hole, adding more pressure. This is just what she needs as she explodes like a firecracker. Her body shakes as her hips continue to pump with a flood of wetness covering my hand. Never letting up on the pressure, I feel her second orgasm as she screams my name.

Knowin' she's primed, I remove my hand and get up to pull my boxer briefs down. My cock's so hard and the tip is slick with precum. Since getting' tested and coming back clean, I don't bother with a condom. I grab my cock and I start to guide myself to her opening, then with one strong hip thrust, I sheath myself deep inside of her. I start to move, making sure I hit her sweet spot as I roll my hips into her.

Hearing her reaction, I fuck her hard and fast, continuing to push in deep to hit that spot that makes her come hard. Her pussy walls starts to flex and tighten around me, so I know she's close. Being behind her, I lean in and suck on her neck while letting my hands roam across her sides to grasp her breasts and squeeze them. They are so sensitive that she gives me that whimper I love so much, telling me she's ready to come all over my cock. So I pull on her nipples and bite down on her neck as I revel in the feel of her pussy, having nothing between us, just skin on skin. It feels fuckin' amazing to feel actually feel her and her excitement directly on me and not through a condom.

I finally send her over the edge as she lets out a scream while her body tightens and her pussy contracts all around me, making me increase my pace now losing my rhythm not that she's reached her peak. As her walls massage my cock her body shakes again right be she comes for a third time.

My cock expands right before the flutter starts. I can feel the hot cum pour out of me and fill her, mixing with release. I continue to pump as I keep coming until I'm empty and there is nothing left.

With Trinity limp as a noodle, we lie entwined together as sleep plays with us. Nothing in my life has ever felt so good and complete. I've finally found what I have always been missing... someone who loves me with all my flaws. Unconditional love at its best.

We spend the remainder of the day in bed, sleeping and making love. The one thing about Trinity being pregnant is that her hormones are making her hornier then even me. I'm being used for sex, but I fuckin' love it. She's actually wearing me out. I slowly get out of bed and say, "We need to eat and get some much-needed fuel before I pass out." Reaching for my jeans, the phone starts to ring.

I grab the cordless with a "Lo." Listening intently, I can see Trinity watch me. My jaw clenches and I know my face is losing its color. "We'll be there as soon as we can. Thanks."

Hangin' up the phone, I say, "Fern was rushed to the hospital. Doc says it isn't good and it's probably best we get there now." She nods and immediately waddles to get up and throw on some clothes. I wait for her in the front room, sitting on the couch with my head in my hands.

She comes in and sits next to me, grabbing one of my hands. "Baby, all I'm going to say right now is don't give up on her, okay?" I look at her with so much pain in my eyes, "Don't give up on her, Cadence. Never give up because she depends on you more than you depend on her. She needs to see your strength, so you show her that."

I pull her in as close as I can and just hold her, no, I hang on to her for dear life. Releasing her, I help her up. "Let's go. We need to be there for the both of them."

As we go to leave, the kittens make their appearance, reminding us both that they haven't been fed yet. I tell Trinity to feed them while I clean out the litter boxes. The pregnancy books say that she shouldn't clean out the litter, so once both kittens are fed and their boxes cleaned, we head out to the hospital.

CHAPTER THIRTY

CADENCE

As minutes turn into hours, we all wait to hear word on Fern. Anything at all. As I look around the waiting area they had us move to it hits me and I realize how loved Fern truly is. Not only are all of the Horde family here, but also some of the town folks that Fern considers friends: Axe, Enforcer, Bear, Stash and Ugly. Yeah, I know, right?

As time goes by, everyone's on edge, not knowing what's going on. Dee has gone to the nurses' station, only to be told that they will tell us something when they know. Dee doesn't take that too well and Des has to hold her back. The tension in her face and the way she keeps wiping tears away gives a brief look into the agony she's in, not knowing what's going on with her best friend.

When the door opens, all eyes shoot up and we're all shocked to see Paula in a wheelchair being pushed in by an intern. Immediately Axe pushes through the crowd to her side. "Sweetheart, I told you to stay in bed and I would be by when we had news. You need your rest, honey."

Paula gives him a look that would kill a weaker man. "Real nice, Bad Dog. You really know how to keep things on the down low, don't you?" Everyone looks confused at what she just called him. "You need to remember that you don't own me. I'm my own person. Just because we share space doesn't give you the right to tell me what to do, got it?"

Axe actually smiles, and even as guy, from one hot guy to another I'll admit that he's a handsome guy when he smiles, even showing off his dimples. "Sweetheart, we share more than space, and if you don't want me to embarrass you in front of all these God-fearing folks, behave."

A couple of chuckles and snickers can be heard from the peanut gallery on the one side of the room and Paula turns to glare at the three Asphalt Riders before she almost spits the words out to Axe, "Don't be an asshole in front of your boys. You don't want to embarrass me? How about I tell your buddies what you were doing last weekend at my place, huh? What do you think about that? Hey, guys, you won't believe what Bad Dog was doing at my apartment especially when he—"

Axe's hand is over her mouth as he leans in, whispering, "Stalemate, my sweets." He moves her hair away from the side, turning her face to his and plants one hot smooch on her parted lips.

The room goes back to their waiting as Axe gets Paula comfortable on the small couch, while the kids get up to let her rest on it. He sits next to her, pulling her closer so she can lift her legs up on the couch, slightly lying down, using Axe as a pillow.

It seems like forever to me when finally, the doctor enters the waiting room looking around. "Who's here for Fern Murphy?" We all start speaking at once as the doctor shakes his head.

Doc walks in behind him, looking totally exhausted. "Dr. King, this is Fern's extended family, so you can tell them anything."

The doctor turns to our little group of misfits in the room and begins to fill us in, "Fern was lucky to get in when she did. Her port was infected so we had to surgically remove it and flush it out. She's on intravenous antibiotics and will be staying here for at least a couple of days. Her counts are off, and we will eventually have to put in another port. The problem is that all her veins are collapsing, so it's making it hard to find a good one. Besides that, she is very dehydrated and weak. I explained to Gabriel that her window of using a viable bone marrow transplant is closing quickly."

I have to ask, "What are you sayin', Dr. King? Is Fern not gonna make it? Is she dying? Are you saying that there is nothin' we can do?" Trinity moves to my side.

My body tenses as we wait for the answer. "Son, she's probably the worst she has ever been since we started to treat her. Fern's body is starting to shut down and that is tying our hands. We're trying to keep her as comfortable as we can."

As Dr. King finishes, Des reaches for Gabriel as he slumps forward. Trying to hold the bear of a man up is nearly impossible until the guys from both MC clubs come and give him a hand.

Dr. King stays for a while, answering all of our questions. When he turns to leave, he looks back at Doc and tells him, "I have the staff moving a bed into Fern's room for you, and I also ordered a tray for you. Use the shower in her room as there will be some scrubs you can change into."

Watchin' him leave, no one knows what to say as we just stare at each other until Doc speaks up, "Fern would be so overwhelmed to know that you all came here for her. She would say something like, '*I know you are all so busy, but it means the world to me that you are here,*' and I double that. Never have I felt so much love from people who don't share blood ties. Got no words that can express my gratitude for all of your support, no matter how bad this looks and turns out. I'm out of ideas and now all I have left is to pray to God that he watches over my girl."

At this last comment, I burst from Trinity's side to get right up in Doc's face. "Don't give up on her, Doc. Don't you dare give up on her, not ever." Des and Wolf come to pull me back as Doc shakes his head and pulls me to his chest, arms around my shoulders. As he continues to hold me close, his shoulders start to shake, and I hold on to Doc for dear life. Everyone looks away giving us our moment. When I finally pull away, I go straight for the door without a word to anyone, not even Trinity.

CHAPTER THIRTY-ONE

CADENCE

I quietly enter Fern's room with the nurse's eyes on me. Well, her eyes are actually checkin' me out, giving me an invitation. Which pisses me off Fuck, even now at a time like this, bitches can be crass. I just turn away from her invitation and walk toward the bed. She looks so small and frail in the hospital bed, hooked up to a bunch of machines.

I sit in the chair on the side of the bed, lifting her fragile hand in mine. I can feel her pulse because she is so thin. Tears start in the corner of my eyes but not wantin' to upset her, I go to wipe my eyes as she turns her head. She squeezes my hand with the little bit of strength she has and tries to smile at me, "Cadence, honey. Don't cry for me. However, this ends, I want you to be happy and not sad. I've lived every dream of mine, except to have a baby, and we know that will never happen now."

"Fern, I don't know what to do for you. You know I

would give my life for you. I prayed that I would be a match for you. I don't understand any of it." I try so hard to hold in the emotional heartache, but the tears roll down my cheeks regardless. I look at the woman who actually saved my life and gave me a reason to live. Her kindness and beautiful heart drew me to her, and a friendship was born that has grown over the years. She has never judged me, even during my wildest times. She's been my constant. No judgement just giving her love.

As the years went by, I saw Fern as a second mom. Realizing I might actually lose her, I feel my heart break. I start to feel my anxiety kick in, and then I feel Trinity's warm hands on my shoulders. Before turnin' around, I glance at Fern who has a brilliant smile on her gaunt face.

Trinity leans in and whispers in my ear, "Baby, remember you have to be her strength right now. She needs every bit of it to get through this. Don't give up on her just yet. She's a fighter." Reaching back, I pull her around and sit her directly on my lap.

Fern starts to giggle softly, but it turns into a genuine laugh even if her breathing is a bit off. Her face is tinged with a pink hue and her eyes seem to sparkle from within. I pull Trinity closer, placing my head on her shoulder so only she can hear me say, "Thank you, babe. You're just what Fern needs. You are what we both need in our lives; a ray of sunshine that shines brightly, bringin' everyone out of the dark and into your light. I sure do love you, Trinity."

As she hangs her head down so I don't see the blush on her face, I see Fern with tears in her eyes as she listens to my words to Trinity. Fern nods her head and places her hand on her heart, pumping it up then down. I know exactly what she means as she used to do that when I refused to speak. That was her way of telling me she loved me, no matter what. I can't lose her, no matter what they have to do.

"Cadence, you've been a joy in my life from the start. I have never met anyone with such an inner strength and will to live. Never lose that quality within yourself. I have always told you if it's worth having, then it's worth fighting for. Remember back when you were finally able to confide in me about your childhood, and all the bad things that happened? Life is full of struggles and even though both of you have had your share, I've a feeling more are coming your way, especially you, Cadence. Both you and Gabriel have been doing a wonderful job trying to take care of me, but I'm so tired, Cadence."

"I don't like where this is going Fern, so stop. I won't accept anything but you gettin' better and being around to see our baby. We need you to be here." The tremor can be heard in my voice, but I don't care. "I can't do this by myself, without you. Please don't stop fighting don't leave me."

"Cadence, it's now in God's hands. Man has done all he can for me. With all the work and effort put into the charity ride, we couldn't find a donor, and I see that as another sign from above. I'm preparing you because there will come a time when both of my men will need to say goodbye to me. Don't let me go without a proper sendoff, you hear me, honey?" Even though I know she's trying to make light of this situation, I'm not going for it.

"No, I refuse to say goodbye, Fern. It ain't happening."

She slowly shakes her head. "As hard as this will be, I need you to promise to look out for Gabriel when I'm gone. He is going to have an extremely hard time with this and he'll need all of you. Tell me you'll watch over him and have his back, Cadence. I know it will also be hard for you, but with Trinity at your side, you will be able to move on faster than my Gabriel."

I hear a sound like water hittin' the floor. I look over at Trinity, who has a dazed expression on her face as she looks between her legs. "Oh my God I just peed my pants and I couldn't stop it. I'm so embarrassed."

At this, Fern lets out a loud scream, "Gabriel, Gabriel!" The door bursts open as Doc, Des and Dee run in. "Trinity's water broke."

CHAPTER THIRTY-TWO

CADENCE

When Fern's words reach my ears, I immediately panic. "What the fuck? Is it really time?" I watch as her face twitches with pain. This is all so sudden. I thought these things took time, but she's already having contractions from the look of pain on her face. "Baby, breathe. Come on, just like in that class we took. You have to breathe through the contractions. I'm right here, Trinity, and I ain't leaving, so just try to relax. Des, get a fuckin' doctor in here. She's going into labor."

All of sudden, Trinity's eyes widen as another contraction kicks in. "Cadence, it hurts so bad and it's happening so fast!"

Reaching for her hands, I squeeze them, looking into her eyes. "Trinity, I have total faith that not only can you do this, but you will. If our baby wants to make its entrance early, then dammit, we can't stop it. Let's try the breathing again, in and out. Come on, Trinity, breathe with me, slowly. In then out, you can do it.

You're one of the strongest women I have ever met. That's it, baby. See, you got this. We can get through this."

As the door opens, an orderly appears with a wheelchair. Between Des, Doc, and me, we get her into the chair. As soon as she's settled, another contraction hits so we wait for it to pass. Then the orderly pushes Trinity out of the room, telling all of us following him that they are headed to the labor and delivery floor.

~Dee Dee~

I look over to Fern who has tears in her eyes. "Sweetie, she'll be just fine. Women have been having babies for years." At my words, Fern's tears turn in to sobs. I rush over and pull Fern to me. "Are you in pain? Do I need to get a nurse? What is the matter, Fern?"

"I'll never experience that, Dee Dee. Even if I beat this frigging cancer, I have been told my chances to have a baby are little to none. We did freeze some of my eggs, but that is also a one in a million chance. I'm so happy for Cadence and Trinity, but there is a little bit of envy on my part. To be able to feel a baby growing inside of you, moving, and kicking and then going through the miracle of birth is something I've wanted my entire life. I never wanted to be a career woman. All my dreams were about finding my soul mate, getting married, and then when the time was right, starting a family and having a bunch of kids. Well, we see how great that worked out, didn't we?"

Not having any words to make it better, I just hold my friend during this dark time in her life. I wouldn't change anything because I love my kids. My heart breaks for Fern because her life has been a constant battle. I've prayed that Fern would beat the cancer and somehow find a way to have the family she always wanted.

Fern finally pulls it together somewhat and I let her go to lie back on the bed. "Dee Dee, never tell Gabriel about this mini breakdown. He has tried everything to make my life the best it could possibly be. Even before the cancer, when we were trying to get pregnant, it never happened. I just pray Gabriel doesn't feel like I failed him as his woman and a wife."

"Fern, you know that he loves you with his entire heart. With or without children, you have made his life the best it could ever be, just like you make everyone around you feel so very special and loved. I need you to calm down and relax. It isn't good for you to get upset. Do you want some water? Maybe some hot tea? I can ring the nurse for anything you want."

Fern raises her head. "Some hot tea actually sounds really good, Dee. Thanks."

CHAPTER THIRTY-THREE

CADENCE

"Well, she's still in labor. Cadence is going crazy back there. Wolf, maybe you should go back and give him some support because I ain't cuttin' it. If he continues to cuss me out, he'll be unconscious when his kid is born." At my words, there are some giggles, and the bikers laugh out loud at the frustration in my words.

"Do you think it's okay for me to go back there, being that I'm not related to either of them?"

At his words, I glance at Cadence's family in the corner, who I called as soon as Trinity went into labor. They all smile back at us as Ruthie replies, "Wolf, he considers you one of his brothers and over the years, you guys have built a solid friendship. He needs someone he can relate to who has been part of his life. No hard feelings, Wolf, go to him and help him out. Trinity is probably losing her mind with him going off at everyone. He never was the most patient boy, and I can see that has followed him into manhood."

I raise my eyebrows at Wolf. "Any other excuses for not going back there? I get the feeling that you're stalling, Wolf. Get back there, now." Wolf shakes his head and heads out the door.

"Des, we have a pool. What do you think? Boy or girl?" Enforcer yells across the room.

"Dude, I have no fuckin' idea. Who started the pool anyway?"

Enforcer shifts his eyes and then under his breath, he says, "Trinity, dude, that's who."

For a minute the room is shockingly quiet, then we all burst out into laughter. Leave it to Trinity to start her own pool on the sex of her own child. She has come a long way over these past months and her personality is taking shape as a very smart sassy woman who is starting to love life.

Minutes turn to hours as we all wait for the baby to make its entrance. Stash and Bear went for a pizza run, and everyone is eating as Wolf comes back in the room with a worried look on his face. "They are taking Trinity to delivery right now. The baby was breach and they have worked for six hours now, trying to turn the baby. They have finally done it, so they are ready to push her along now. Shit, you all should have seen Cadence's face. I think he is going to gut the doctor. He's getting' into some scrubs and they are preparing her for whatever needs to be done."

~Wolf~

"Mr. Wolf? We need to get you in some scrubs as Mr. Powers is asking for you to be in there, too."

"What did you say? And my name is Wolf, just Wolf, miss."

As the nurse repeats herself, my shoulders are shaking and obviously Axe sees this because he walks to me and places his hand on my trembling shoulder. "Brother, he needs you. Don't think about it, just do it."

I look up to Axe and see the sincerity in his eyes, so I give him a nod. As I walk out the door, I turn and make a quiet request to the group of people in the room. "Say a prayer that this baby is born healthy, and everything turns out okay."

I struggle to get into the scrubs the nice nurse handed me. She watches me try to get into the pants and leaves the room, returning with another set, "Try these on. They're a bigger size and should make it easier for you," Thanking her, I then turn my back, pulling on the scrubs with ease. After I'm covered, she leads me down a hallway through a couple of doors and hands me a mask. "Put this on. We are entering the surgical room now." I place it on my face as I'm hit with a brightly lit room. Trinity is lying on a gurney under another bright light as Cadence is on her right side in a chair, holding her hand.

He looks up, seeing me approach. The relief in Cadence's eyes lets me know that Axe was right. Cadence needs me.

"Thank God, dude. Didn't think you'd come back

here. We are both freakin' the fuck out man. Thanks for bein' here, Wolf. I need ya, brother."

"I'm always here for you, little brother, you know that, but you okay with me in here, seeing your woman give birth? If the roles were reversed, there's no way in Hell I'd be okay with it."

"No, Wolf. You ain't checkin' out my baby's momma, no matter what. Keep your eyes up here. Ya get to the other side hold Trin's hand and be part of your godchild's birth, that's it, man. Got it?"

I laugh, which catches Trinity's attention. "Little one, are you good with me in here during this special time?"

She smiles softly. "Who do you think sent the nurse for you? He," she points at Cadence, "is driving me crazy, and the only way we are going to be able to handle this is if you keep him calm. That's all I am asking and don't hold anything against me during the labor because I am not responsible for what comes out of my mouth." We all laugh, which helps bring down our stress.

Suddenly, Trinity lurches in the bed. "Holy fuck, this shit hurts. When do I get my epidural? I can't wait any longer. Cadence, get me the damn shot, now." Cadence and I look at the angel on the gurney in shock. Trinity barely swears and now she has a trucker's mouth. I think to myself, *this is going to be a long night.*

After the doctor has her prepped, things start to move quickly. Trinity received her epidural, which helped her immensely with the pain. Both Cadence and I helped her with the breathing techniques. As time went on, I helped position her when she needed to reposition herself, and Cadence rubbed her back when the pressure, even with the shot, was too much.

Finally, at 2:32 a.m., the baby crowned. I took the side away from the mirror as they lifted the bed with Cadence's help. The doctor kept checking Trinity under the sheet and as each contraction came, instructed her on what to do. Cadence held her hand as I wiped her forehead and face. When it was time, the doctor looked up at Cadence first, then Trinity. "Trinity, on the next contraction, I want you to push as hard as you can. Cadence, come here so you can see the head."

Cadence walks around and the look on his face is priceless. I watch my friend as every emotion passes over his face until it's of just plain awe. Trinity lets out a moan and Cadence rushes to her side. When the doctor tells her to push, she starts to bear down and push with all her might as her face turns bright red and she gasps for air. When the contraction passes, the doctor once again instructs Trinity, "We are almost there. This next contraction, give it your all and push as hard as you can."

She nods as she squeezes Cadence's hand until it turns white. He lets out a howl as I lean into her. "Little one, let go, he will need both of his hands to change this baby's diapers." She loosens her hold and giggles at my words.

At the start of the next contraction, Trinity leans

her head up and bears down. Beads of perspiration pop up on her forehead as her upper body trembles with her efforts. The doctor encourages her, "Come on, Trinity, that's it. You're doing great. One more push and this baby will be out, so give it everything you've got."

With one final effort, Trinity falls to the bed as they hear the doctor announce the baby is out. As we wait patiently, the doctor holds the baby up as it starts to cry loudly. "Trinity and Cadence, meet your daughter."

Trinity looks at Cadence and breaks into sobs. Grabbing her face he asks, "Baby, what's the matter? Are you in pain?"

She reaches out and caresses his face. "Cadence, I hope you didn't have your heart set on a son."

"Trinity, never worry about that, baby. We have a beautiful, healthy miracle and that is all that matters. Darlin', we have a daughter and hopefully she has your beauty and intelligence." The doctor asks Cadence if he wants to cut the cord, so he walks over.

Trinity glances at me as I watch her closely. "Trinity, you're such a special woman. I'll never forget this moment, so thank you for including me. Cadence is such a lucky man. Thank you again, little one."

She holds my hand to her heart. "I never had a brother, but from the moment I met you, the connection was there. I'm so glad that you're here to meet your goddaughter, Wolf. We owe you for our lives, never forget that. No matter what, we'll always be here for you as you have been for us."

As Cadence approaches her side, he has the baby in his arms. Tears are running down his cheeks. "Let me introduce you to your daughter. She's so beautiful, just like you. I love you, baby." He leans in and we both get our first look at their daughter. She has a ton of dark hair, just like Cadence. Her skin is rosy with a button nose. As Trinity holds the baby, a nurse comes over to help her breastfeed the little girl. At this, I step back, telling Cadence, "I will go let the others know that the *Little Princess* has arrived."

Turning, I leave them to enjoy this special moment together. The three of them. Walking to the changing area, I remove the scrubs then head to the waiting room. Entering, I see the same people still sitting exactly where they were hours ago. Even Doc and Fern are here. Fern is in a wheelchair, bundled up in blankets.

Once they see me, they all look up at me expectantly. "I'm proud to announce that after much fuss, the baby has arrived."

Des asks the obvious question, "So, what did they have? Is it a boy or a girl? Is it healthy?"

"The baby is definitely healthy and blessed with some strong lungs. It's a girl, Des, so yeah the *Little Princess* has arrived."

Cheers and laughter follow my announcement. I watch as Doc gently holds Fern as she quietly cries into his shoulder.

~Trinity~

"Trinity, we're gonna have to name our little angel. Do you have any names?" I shake my head as the nurse takes the baby back to clean her up.

I watch the nurse until I can't see the baby, then I look to Cadence. "How about you, Cadence? Any name you like or want? Maybe your mom's or grandma's?"

He shakes his head. I think for a moment, then suggest to him, "How about naming her after Fern? She means a lot to you, and I have come to love her myself. It'll show her how much we care about her."

"As much as I love Fern, I don't want the baby to be named after her. It makes it feel like she is dyin' or dead already, and I don't want that thought out there, but how about Hope Fern Powers? It sounds good, doesn't it?"

I smile widely, "I love it, babe. That's it our baby girl's name, Hope Fern Powers."

CHAPTER THIRTY-FOUR

CADENCE

As we wait for our baby girl to be brought back to us, the doctor starts speaking about the umbilical cord and placenta while placing it in a storage container that I didn't notice until now. I'm watching how carefully everyone is being with gloves and dry ice as the doctor tells the nurse to call the Bone Marrow Bank, that they have it ready for pick up. Just as I'm about to ask what in the fuck is going on, I feel Trinity's hand reaching for mine. I look away for a moment from all the action taking place at one of the surgical tables and that cooler thingy.

"Baby, I don't want you to get angry, but I've been keeping something from you," she starts. "After the charity ride, when all of the donations to the Bone Marrow Registry were in and no matches were found for Fern, I started to look up online what else we could do for Fern. That is when I discovered that the umbilical cord blood and placenta could be used for a transplant. There are some issues because there isn't a lot of matter, oh, I mean blood, for them to use. Doctor, can you explain this to Cadence because I can't even pronounce the words that I've read about."

Turning sharply to face the doctor, I listen to him explain about three types of stem cell transplants, telling me of how each and every one of them works and how they use them and I'm in shock. Feeling like I'm going to pass out, I grab for the gurney as Trinity yells, "Holy crap. Catch him, he's gonna pass out."

All eyes turn to me as my knees buckle and I slide to the floor, still hanging onto the bar of the bed. Two nurses come to my side, one with a cold wet cloth, and the other with smelling salts. After a couple of minutes of just sittin' there, they help me to my feet, putting my ass in a chair next to Trinity.

Finally able to talk and not knowing where to start, I just ask, "Fuck, Trinity. Why didn't you talk to me about this? I don't understand the secrecy as this is a good thing, right? I'm so fuckin' confused, baby, talk to me please."

Trying to move to get closer to the side of the bed, I notice the pain cross her face and realize with a start that this woman just went through labor and delivery to give me a miracle.

Regardless of why she didn't share this with me, her intentions were, as always, about helping someone else. Clearing her throat, she explains her thoughts to me, "With everything that has been going on, I didn't want to burden you with a Hail Mary for Fern. We don't know if it'll even work or take, but the lady at the Registry was willing to work with me while she made sure everything was in order. I didn't understand all the requirements for them to even consider the baby's blood, not to mention my health had to be in tiptop order. So, we passed with flying colors, and they know how serious this is, as Fern needs this immediately. That's why they are taking it for testing to see if there is a match or partial match. This is our only prayer right now, honey, and I had to try. For Fern and Doc, they deserve to be as happy as we are."

"Thanks so much, baby. I don't have the right words to tell you how much this means to me. I don't want to lose Fern, and if this saves her, that means our baby girl, little Hope, will live up to her name. If it doesn't, at least we tried. You give me such hope, Trinity, that at this moment, I look around and see the true miracle I have in you and Hope. I love ya, baby, so fuckin' much. Look at me, I'm becomin' a pussy, do not tell Wolf and Des. I'll never live this shit down."

As I finish, I hear the magical sound of Trinity giggling at my words. "I won't say a word, but you will owe me, and when I call in my marker, you have to do whatever I say, no questions or whining. Deal?"

"Baby, anything you say."

CHAPTER THIRTY-FIVE

TRINITY

As everyone tries to squeeze into the room to get their first look at our baby, all I see is Fern sitting on the recliner and a mask over her mouth to try and prevent any spreading of germs. Once everyone is settled, Cadence reaches over, picking up little Hope in his arms. Moving the blanket off her sleeping angelic face, he turns to his family, announcing in a husky voice, "We would like to introduce all of ya to our daughter, Hope Fern Powers."

Watching Fern's face at the mention of her name, we all see every emotion possible cross her face.

When she finally looks up at him, her eyes are wet with unshed tears. "Why, Cadence? That poor child being stuck with such a nasty name."

"Our baby needs to start life with the name of a person we are proud to have in our lives. She will grow up with your strength, my mom's love of life, Dee Dee's ability to solve anything that comes her way, Willow's grace, and Daisy's innocence. Each woman in her life will give her gifts to help her in the journey of finding herself."

A loud, "Okay, jerkoff. What about me?" Archie asks sarcastically.

"Oh, right. Hopefully she doesn't take after you with the piercings, tats, and hair color," Cadence finishes on a laugh. Everyone joins in except Archie, who stands and starts for the door. Cadence reaches over, pulling her to him. "I do hope she gets your compassion, ability to always have someone's back, no matter what, and your best trait, which is your humor."

She is taken aback by his words but manages a small smile. He reaches over to squeeze her shoulder. "Sweetie, you are so much more than you think you are. One day, I hope you see what we've all seen for years."

Cadence sits on the edge of the bed and begins with our news, "We'd like to share something that Trinity has been workin' on. To be honest, it was even a surprise to me a few hours ago, and this has to do to with Hope." Looking down, he reverently caresses our daughter's peaches and cream cheek. "And with Fern. At this point, I am going turn it over to Trinity to explain, as this was all her idea."

I try to sit up straighter in the bed and look around the room. "I don't know how I got so lucky to be a part of this wonderful group. You guys are now my family. With everything going on in our lives, and all the crap we've dealt with in the past couple of weeks, please know that each and every one of you're part of my heart. Not only because you saved me from my abusive life, but accepted me for me. After the ride, and when the Registry told us that even though the donations received were helping others, there were no matches for Fern, I started to do some research on transplants, including bone marrow, and then stem cells. What surprised me is that I found something that might be the answer to all of our prayers. Umbilical cord blood can be used in transplants, as can blood from the placenta. I contacted Des's contact at the Registry, and she worked with me so that when we had the baby, they could capture the cord and placenta, put it on ice, and at this moment, they are testing to see if it will be a match for Fern. Now, before ya'll get crazy, from what I was told, it doesn't have to be a total match. It can be a… crap, Cadence. What did the doctor call it?"

"Something like allog? I don't know, babe. There is too much shit is goin' on in my head. Feels like it's in a vise. Sorry."

"No, that's it! It is an allogeneic transplant! That means it isn't a total match, but they can still use it."

Dee speaks up, "How did you know to do this, Trinity? What made you even look for other options?"

As Dee finishes, Willow quietly adds in, "This won't hurt baby Hope, will it? I mean, what happens if she needs that blood for something. Don't parents freeze that for the future?"

Doc comes and gently sits on the edge of the bed while reaching for me. He encloses my entire body in what I can only describe as a bear hug. Holding me close, he whispers softly for my ears only, "Baby girl, your full heart and your thoughtfulness for my Fern will be with me until my dying day. Know how much Cadence, you, and that little angel mean to us. You're the daughter Fern has never had, don't you forget that sweetheart." Kissing my cheek, he gets up and moves to Fern, who is just staring at me.

"Trinity, you did this for me? I appreciate it, but we have to accept that even after all the treatments, the cancer has won. I love all of you, but there comes a time when even that emotion we value so much isn't going to be enough. The time is coming and I'll need all of you to accept that I'm going to die. It won't be pretty, and sure, it won't be quick, so I'll need everyone's strength for my next journey, so don't be upset. I've come to accept my fate. But I will need all of you to take care of my Gabriel after I'm gone."

After that statement, Doc finally has his say, "Fern I know this has been extremely hard on you but we are not giving up. Trinity is giving you, no us, a second chance. Please, baby, don't pass it up. Let's take it one day at a time, please. I can't live without you. Please think about us and what time we could still have together. Look at that baby. She could be our last hope."

~Fern~

As Hope looks my way, I feel warmth in my body that hasn't been there for a long time. It continues to warm me from the inside out. As I find myself so immersed with the baby's stare; I don't hear what Cadence asks. Turning to look his way, the moment my eyes move, the warmth vanishes. Looking back to Hope, I feel the warmth return. I'm slowly freaking out until I see baby Hope yawn and close her eyes. This time, the warmth stays with me. Doc pulls me to his side whispering, "Don't give up on us, baby. Please don't. I wouldn't have anything to live for if you weren't here."

Hearing the emotion in his voice, I once again look at the baby who is now sleeping. Knowing that deep down my fears of any kind of wishful thinking that this could work and that I'm afraid of putting my faith into this and it doesn't work it hits me I'm getting a last chance. I reach for Trinity's hand, giving it a squeeze. "Well, Trinity. If you're willing to go through all of this work and trouble for me, then I guess the least I can do is try and have *hope*." At my words, everyone lets out a nervous laugh.

I look at the sleeping baby and softly continue, "Thank you, baby Hope, for giving me back the ability to have faith, take a chance, put myself out there one more time. I'll give it a try and pray that it works. All we can do right now."

As everyone claps and laughs, baby Hope opens her eyes and I'm positive the little girl actually smiles at me.

(Fern)

Watching my husband and Des leave, the feeling in the room changes. For a split second, after Trinity shared her secret with all of us, I felt some renewed faith and hope that maybe there is a chance I could beat this awful disease. But watching Gabriel almost lose it before he exited, something deep inside me felt his pain. My poor Gabriel has been through hell and back with all that has happened to me. Why he is still with me, I have no idea

Dee Dee approaches my bedside. "Fern, he will be just fine, probably needing some air to take in all this information. How you holding up?"

"I'm trying to stay positive, but just knowing this is my last effort scares the crap out of me. What happens if it doesn't work? Where does that leave me?"

"You heard what the doctor told you, Fern, you have to stay positive and keep fighting. They wouldn't be going through with the transplant if they didn't think it would work."

Nodding her way, I sit up in my hospital bed gazing at all of my "family," or as Des calls it, the Horde, my weary body starts to fail me. Exhausted beyond my limits, I try to stay focused on what everyone is saying, even though it is coming across mumbled and unclear. I know my pain pump just released a dose of morphine because I am getting that foggy feeling. After a couple of minutes go by, I give Dee Dee a look. As I try to get more comfortable, Dee Dee's sharp eyes take me in. After watching and observing me for a minute she looks around the room, telling everyone it's time to go and let me rest. I nod in her direction as the drugs start to work, knowing I will be asleep in no time at all.

One by one they come to me and give me a kiss or a hand squeeze. I try to stay focused, but when it's Daisy's turn, she looks pale with dark circles under her eyes.

"You doing okay, sweetie?" Her eyes shoot up to meet mine and before she can hide it, I see the pain in her eyes. "Daisy, what's going on? Talk to me please. You're worrying me."

Her eyes shift to see if anyone is listening, especially her mom, Dee Dee.

"Nothing is wrong, Fern. Everything is great." She tries to make her tone sound happy but doesn't come close to succeeding.

"Kiddo, look at me. No matter what I am going through, I'm always here for you, sweetie. Okay?"

She nods, leaning in, giving me a soft kiss, then turns, walking out of the room looking like she has the weight of the world on her shoulders.

By the time Cadence gets to me, I am fighting to keep my eyes open. He leans down, whispering in my ear, "No matter what, I'm not lettin' ya go, Fern. Don't stop fighting, 'cause Hope needs you in her life just like Trinity and I do."

Kissing my forehead, he gently caresses my cheek, moving aside for Trinity to give me a peck also. As she leans toward me, I feel intense warmth in my body suddenly, and struggling with opening my eyes I see little Hope staring at me intently. This has to be the drugs playing with me because, I swear, she just smiled at me. As Trinity turns to Cadence and they head out of the room, they take that warmth with them.

Suddenly I feel chilled. Dee Dee sees me trembling and grabs another blanket, placing it over me. Sitting on the edge of my bed, she holds my hand softly as she speaks to me.

"Go ahead and sleep, my friend. I will watch over you until Gabriel and Des return. Sweet dreams."

Squeezing her hand, I glance her way and put to words what is weighing on my mind.

"Worried about Daisy, Dee Dee. Something is up with her. Can't put my finger on it, but you need to keep an eye on her. Is she having problems in school? She isn't herself and you know how mean kids can be, Dee Dee."

"I noticed some subtle things too, Fern. Spoke to Des about it, but with everything going on I haven't had the time to sit her down and speak to her. I will rectify that as soon as I can. She's distant and seems to want to be by herself more lately. She isn't active in her usual activities either, now that I think of it. This will be addressed, Fern, promise. Now, back to you. How you doing?"

"Dee Dee, I am so scared. I don't want to die but I can feel my body giving up. Trying to hang on and after what Trinity just..."

I take a moment to catch my breath. Dee Dee brings a cup of water with a straw to my lips and graciously I take a couple of sips to moisten my mouth.

"I am so grateful to Trinity for all she has put together. Believe me, praying it works, but if Hope and I don't match that is my last hope."

Looking at her I kind of giggle, "No pun intended" as she smiles at me. Dee Dee clears her throat and gives it to me direct, as she always does.

"Fern, you can't lose faith. This is a miracle in itself with Trinity having the baby and thinking to look into an umbilical cord stem cell transplant. I have a good feeling on this and totally believe in the power of prayer. We will start the prayer circle and I know God will hear us, as you have been through enough. But it is all on your shoulders, my friend, you must continue to fight and this is the biggest fight of your life. Honey, you have to want to live, that's the only way you will get through this and live. Now can you do that for me, Fern, can you fight like you never have before? We will all support you, but you got to do this for yourself because that's the only way you will get through this."

Yawning as I pull the covers up to my neck, thinking on her words, I glance at my longtime friend, squeezing her hand with what little strength I have left.

"Dee Dee, I swear to you on everything I hold precious that I will battle this with everything I have left. But I need you to promise me that if this doesn't work, or it fails, and I lose this battle, please watch out for my Gabriel. He'll need all of you to support him because I don't think he will be able to handle it."

As tears start to slowly run down her cheeks, she reaches over, squeezing my shoulder.

"That isn't going to happen, so no need for me to promise that. We always have each other's back, sweetie, you know that."

Knowing she is trying to put me off, I actually feel a bit upset as I again request.

"Dee, that aside, I need that promise. Without me, Gabriel only has the Horde and I need to know in my heart that if something does happen you will watch out for him, support him, and eventually help him to move on and continue living. Knowing him, he will lock down and let his life pass him by and I don't want that. So here and now, please give me your word that you will make sure he truly lives and not only exists. He deserves to have love and have a family in his life, if it is with me or someone else eventually."

She slowly turns away from me for a minute, trying to compose herself and softly replies to my request.

"Fern, the last thing I want to think about is you not being here and Gabriel moving on, but if that is what you want, then I will promise you that if the unthinkable happens, I will honor your wishes and support Gabriel in his time of need. Okay?"

I just nod my head.

Dee Dee can see that I am fighting the effect of the medicine and starts running her hands through my hair gently.

"Sweet Fern, go ahead and sleep my friend. I am here for you always and will watch over you until both Gabriel and Des return."

As I fall into a drug-induced sleep, my mind takes me back to Gabriel's and my first encounter.

Continue with Gabriel 'Doc' and Fern's story in Gabriel's Treasure (Book 3).

Thank you for taking the time to read Cadence and Trinity's story. Their story has a happily ever after but not everyone is so lucky. Even though this is a fictional story the story line unfortunately is not.

Sexual Assault and Abuse is increasing daily in the United States.

If you or someone you know is in such a situation please talk to someone at your church or school. Go to the police or a hospital. Seek assistance immediately and do not remain in the situation as

it will only get worse.

Please know that there are resources out there to assist you in any situation. I have listed a few on the following page.

SEXUAL ABUSE & ASSAULT RESOURCES

Sexual Abuse

The prevalence of child sexual abuse is difficult to determine because it is often not reported.

Experts agree that the incidence is far greater than what is reported to authorities.

Below represents some of the research done on child sexual abuse.

Studies by David Finkelhor, Director of the Crimes Against Children Research Center, show that:

- 1 in 5 girls and 1 in 20 boys is a victim of child sexual abuse;
- Self-report studies show that 20% of adult females and 5-10% of adult males recall a childhood sexual assault or sexual abuse incident;

- During a one-year period in the U.S., 16% of youth ages 14 to 17 had been sexually victimized;
- Over the course of their lifetime, 28% of U.S. youth ages 14 to 17 had been sexually victimized;
- Children are most vulnerable to CSA between the ages of 7 and 13.

Call *Darkness to Light's* helpline, 1-866-FOR-LIGHT **to be routed to resources in your own community, or call the Child Help USA National Child Abuse Hotline,** 1-800-4-A-CHILD

Sexual Assault
National Sexual Assault Hotline - 1.800.656.HOPE

Remember you are never alone and have places that will help you.

ABOUT THE AUTHOR

USA Today Bestselling author D. M. Earl spins stories about real life situations with characters that are authentic, genuine and sincere. Each story allows the characters to come to life with each turn of the page while they try to find their HEA through much drama and angst.

When not writing, DM loves to read some of her favorite authors books. Also she loves to spend quality time with her hubby & family along with her 7 fur babies. When weather permits she likes to ride her Harley.

Contact D.M at DM@DMEARL.COM
Website: http://www.dmearl.com/

- facebook.com/DMEarlAuthorIndie
- twitter.com/dmearl
- instagram.com/dmearl14
- amazon.com/D-M-Earl/e/B00M2HB12U
- bookbub.com/authors/d-m-earl
- goodreads.com/dmearl
- pinterest.com/dauthor

ALSO BY D.M. EARL

DEVIL'S HANDMAIDENS MC: TIMBER-GHOST, MONTANA CHAPTER
Tink (Book #1)

GRIMM WOLVES MC SERIES
Behemoth (Book 1)
Bottom of the Chains-Prospect (Book 2)
Santa...Nope The Grimm Wolves (Book 3)
Keeping Secrets-Prospect (Book 4)
A Tormented Man's Soul: Part One (Book 5)
Triad Resumption: Part Two (Book 6)

WHEELS & HOGS SERIES
Connelly's Horde (Book 1)
Cadence Reflection (Book 2)
Gabriel's Treasure (Book 3)
Holidays with the Horde (Book 4)
My Sugar (Book 5)
Daisy's Darkness (Book 6)

THE JOURNALS TRILOGY

Anguish (Book 1)

Vengeance (Book 2)

Awakening (Book 3)

STAND ALONE TITLES

Survivor: A Salvation Society Novel

Printed in Great Britain
by Amazon